MALEMUTE KID

THE·SON·OF THE·WOLF

Stories of the Northland

JACK LONDON

Illustrated by Peter Thorpe

Star Rover House

Oakland, California

MCMLXXXI

Copyright © 1981
by
Star Rover House

Library of Congress Catalog Number
ISBN 0-932458-02-5

Hardbound 200 copies.
Softbound 1000 copies.

573

Star Rover House
306-12th Street
Oakland, California 94607

CONTENTS

ILLUSTRATIONS

TO

THE SONS OF THE WOLF

WHO SOUGHT THEIR HERITAGE AND

LEFT THEIR BONES AMONG THE

SHADOWS OF THE

CIRCLE

THE SON OF THE WOLF

THE WHITE SILENCE

"CARMEN won't last more than a couple of days." Mason spat out a chunk of ice and surveyed the poor animal ruefully, then put her foot in his mouth and proceeded to bite out the ice which clustered cruelly between the toes.

"I never saw a dog with a highfalutin' name that ever was worth a rap," he said, as he concluded his task and shoved her aside. "They just fade away and die under the responsibility. Did ye ever see one go wrong with a sensible name like Cassiar, Siwash, or Husky? No, sir! Take a look at Shookum here, he's" —

Snap! The lean brute flashed up, the white teeth just missing Mason's throat.

"Ye will, will ye?" A shrewd clout behind the ear with the butt of the dogwhip stretched the animal in the snow, quivering softly, a yellow slaver dripping from its fangs.

"As I was saying, just look at Shookum, here — he's got the spirit. Bet ye he eats Carmen before the week's out."

"I'll bank another proposition against that," replied Malemute Kid, reversing the frozen bread placed before the fire to thaw. "We'll eat Shookum before the trip is over. What d' ye say, Ruth?"

The Indian woman settled the coffee with a piece of ice, glanced from Malemute Kid to her husband, then at the dogs, but vouchsafed no reply. It was such a palpable truism that none was necessary. Two hundred miles of unbroken trail in prospect, with a scant six days' grub for themselves and none for the dogs, could admit no other alternative. The two men and the woman grouped about the fire and began their meagre meal. The dogs lay in their harnesses, for it was a midday halt, and watched each mouthful enviously.

"No more lunches after to-day," said Malemute Kid. "And we've got to keep a close eye on the dogs, — they're getting vicious. They'd just as soon pull a fellow down as not, if they get a chance."

"And I was president of an Epworth once, and taught in the Sunday school." Having irrelevantly delivered himself of this, Mason fell into a dreamy contemplation of his steaming moccasins, but was aroused by Ruth filling his cup. "Thank God, we've got slathers of tea! I've seen it growing, down in Tennessee. What wouldn't I give for a hot corn pone just now! Never mind, Ruth; you won't starve much longer, nor wear moccasins either."

The woman threw off her gloom at this, and in her eyes welled up a great love for her white lord, — the first white man she had ever seen, — the first man whom she had known to treat a woman as something better than a mere animal or beast of burden.

"Yes, Ruth," continued her husband, having recourse to the macaronic jargon in which it was alone possible for them to understand each other; "wait till we clean up and pull for the Outside. We'll take the White Man's canoe and go to the Salt Water. Yes, bad water, rough water, — great mountains dance up and down all the time. And so big, so far, so far away, — you travel ten sleep, twenty sleep, forty sleep " (he graphically enumerated the days on his fingers), " all the time water, bad water.   Then you come to great village, plenty people, just the same mosquitoes next summer.   Wigwams oh, so high, — ten, twenty pines.   Hi-yu skookum ! "

He paused impotently, cast an appealing glance at Malemute Kid, then laboriously placed the twenty pines, end on end, by sign language.   Malemute Kid smiled with cheery cynicism ; but Ruth's eyes were wide with wonder, and with pleasure ; for she half believed he was joking, and such condescension pleased her poor woman's heart.

" And then you step into a — a box, and pouf ! up you go."   He tossed his empty cup in the air by way of illustration, and as he deftly caught it, cried : " And biff ! down you come.   Oh, great medicine-men !   You go Fort Yukon, I go Arctic City, — twenty-five sleep, — big string, all the time, — I catch him string, — I say, ' Hello, Ruth ! How are ye ? ' — and you say, ' Is that my good husband ? ' — and I say ' Yes,' — and you say, ' No can bake good bread, no more soda,' — then I say, ' Look in cache, under flour; good-by.' You look and catch plenty soda. All the time you Fort Yukon, me Arctic City. Hi-yu medicine-man!"

Ruth smiled so ingenuously at the fairy story, that both men burst into laughter. A row among the dogs cut short the wonders of the Outside, and by the time the snarling combatants were separated, she had lashed the sleds and all was ready for the trail.

"Mush! Baldy! Hi! Mush on!" Mason worked his whip smartly, and as the dogs whined low in the traces, broke out the sled with the gee-pole. Ruth followed with the second team, leaving Malemute Kid, who had helped her start, to bring up the rear. Strong man, brute that he was, capable of felling an ox at a blow, he could not bear to beat the poor animals, but humored them as a dog-driver rarely does, — nay, almost wept with them in their misery.

"Come, mush on there, you poor sore-footed brutes!" he murmured, after several ineffectual attempts to start the load. But his patience was at last rewarded, and though whimpering with pain, they hastened to join their fellows.

No more conversation ; the toil of the trail will not permit such extravagance. And of all deadening labors, that of the Northland trail is the worst. Happy is the man who can weather a day's travel at the price of silence, and that on a beaten track.

And of all heart-breaking labors, that of breaking trail is the worst. At every step the great webbed shoe sinks till the snow is level with the knee. Then up, straight up, the deviation of a fraction of an inch being a certain precursor of disaster, the snowshoe must be lifted till the surface is cleared ; then forward, down, and the other foot is raised perpendicularly for the matter of half a yard. He who tries this for the first time, if haply he avoids bringing his shoes in dangerous propinquity and measures not his length on the treacherous footing, will give up exhausted at the end of a hundred yards ; he who can keep out of the way of the dogs for a whole day may well crawl into his sleeping-bag with a clear conscience and a pride which passeth all understanding ; and he who travels twenty sleeps on the Long Trail is a man whom the gods may envy.

The afternoon wore on, and with the awe,

born of the White Silence, the voiceless travelers bent to their work. Nature has many
tricks wherewith she convinces man of his
finity, — the ceaseless flow of the tides, the
fury of the storm, the shock of the earth-
quake, the long roll of heaven's artillery, —
but the most tremendous, the most stupefy-
ing of all, is the passive phase of the White
Silence. All movement ceases, the sky clears,
the heavens are as brass ; the slightest whis-
per seems sacrilege, and man becomes timid,
affrighted at the sound of his own voice.
Sole speck of life journeying across the
ghostly wastes of a dead world, he trembles
at his audacity, realizes that his is a maggot's
life, nothing more. Strange thoughts arise
unsummoned, and the mystery of all things
strives for utterance. And the fear of death,
of God, of the universe, comes over him, —
the hope of the Resurrection and the Life,
the yearning for immortality, the vain striving of the imprisoned essence, — it is then,
if ever, man walks alone with God.

So wore the day away. The river took a
great bend, and Mason headed his team for
the cut-off across the narrow neck of land.
But the dogs balked at the high bank.

Again and again, though Ruth and Malemute Kid were shoving on the sled, they slipped back. Then came the concerted effort. The miserable creatures, weak from hunger, exerted their last strength. Up — up — the sled poised on the top of the bank; but the leader swung the string of dogs behind him to the right, fouling Mason's snowshoes. The result was grievous. Mason was whipped off his feet; one of the dogs fell in the traces; and the sled toppled back, dragging everything to the bottom again.

Slash! the whip fell among the dogs savagely, especially upon the one which had fallen.

"Don't, Mason," entreated Malemute Kid; "the poor devil's on its last legs. Wait and we'll put my team on."

Mason deliberately withheld the whip till the last word had fallen, then out flashed the long lash, completely curling about the offending creature's body. Carmen — for it was Carmen — cowered in the snow, cried piteously, then rolled over on her side.

It was a tragic moment, a pitiful incident of the trail, — a dying dog, two comrades in anger. Ruth glanced solicitously from man

Mason was whipped off his feet . . .
and the sled toppled back

to man. But Malemute Kid restrained himself, though there was a world of reproach in his eyes, and bending over the dog, cut the traces. No word was spoken. The teams were double-spanned and the difficulty overcome; the sleds were under way again, the dying dog dragging herself along in the rear. As long as an animal can travel, it is not shot, and this last chance is accorded it, — the crawling into camp, if it can, in the hope of a moose being killed.

Already penitent for his angry action, but too stubborn to make amends, Mason toiled on at the head of the cavalcade, little dreaming that danger hovered in the air. The timber clustered thick in the sheltered bottom, and through this they threaded their way. Fifty feet or more from the trail towered a lofty pine. For generations it had stood there, and for generations destiny had had this one end in view, — perhaps the same had been decreed of Mason.

He stooped to fasten the loosened thong of his moccasin. The sleds came to a halt and the dogs lay down in the snow without a whimper. The stillness was weird; not a breath rustled the frost-encrusted forest; the cold and silence of outer space had chilled the heart and smote the trembling lips of nature. A sigh pulsed through the air, — they did not seem to actually hear it, but rather felt it, like the premonition of movement in a motionless void. Then the great tree, burdened with its weight of years and snow, played its last part in the tragedy of life. He heard the warning crash and attempted to spring up, but almost erect, caught the blow squarely on the shoulder.

The sudden danger, the quick death, — how often had Malemute Kid faced it! The pine needles were still quivering as he gave his commands and sprang into action. Nor did the Indian girl faint or raise her voice in idle wailing, as might many of her white sisters. At his order, she threw her weight on the end of a quickly extemporized handspike, easing the pressure and listening to her husband's groans, while Malemute Kid attacked the tree with his axe. The steel rang merrily as it bit into the frozen trunk, each stroke being accompanied by a forced, audible respiration, the " Huh !" "Huh ! " of the woodsman.

At last the Kid laid the pitiable thing that

was once a man in the snow. But worse than his comrade's pain was the dumb anguish in the woman's face, the blended look of hopeful, hopeless query. Little was said; those of the Northland are early taught the futility of words and the inestimable value of deeds. With the temperature at sixty-five below zero, a man cannot lie many minutes in the snow and live. So the sled-lashings were cut, and the sufferer, rolled in furs, laid on a couch of boughs. Before him roared a fire, built of the very wood which wrought the mishap. Behind and partially over him was stretched the primitive fly, — a piece of canvas, which caught the radiating heat and threw it back and down upon him, — a trick which men may know who study physics at the fount.

And men who have shared their bed with death know when the call is sounded. Mason was terribly crushed. The most cursory examination revealed it. His right arm, leg, and back, were broken ; his limbs were paralyzed from the hips ; and the likelihood of internal injuries was large. An occasional moan was his only sign of life.

No hope; nothing to be done. The pitiless night crept slowly by, — Ruth's portion, the despairing stoicism of her race, and Malemute Kid adding new lines to his face of bronze. In fact, Mason suffered least of all, for he spent his time in Eastern Tennessee, in the Great Smoky Mountains, living over the scenes of his childhood. And most pathetic was the melody of his long-forgotten Southern vernacular, as he raved of swimming-holes and coon-hunts and watermelon raids. It was as Greek to Ruth, but the Kid understood and felt, — felt as only one can feel who has been shut out for years from all that civilization means.

Morning brought consciousness to the stricken man, and Malemute Kid bent closer to catch his whispers.

" You remember when we foregathered on the Tanana, four years come next ice-run ? I did n't care so much for her then. It was more like she was pretty, and there was a smack of excitement about it, I think. But d' ye know, I 've come to think a heap of her. She 's been a good wife to me, always at my shoulder in the pinch. And when it comes to trading, you know there is n't her equal. D' ye recollect the time she shot the

Moosehorn Rapids to pull you and me off
that rock, the bullets whipping the water like
hailstones? — and the time of the famine at
Nuklukyeto? — or when she raced the ice-
run to bring the news? Yes, she's been a
good wife to me, better 'n that other one.
Did n't know I'd been there? Never told
you, eh? Well, I tried it once, down in the
States. That's why I'm here. Been raised
together, too. I came away to give her a
chance for divorce. She got it.

"But that's got nothing to do with Ruth.
I had thought of cleaning up and pulling for
the Outside next year, — her and I, — but
it's too late. Don't send her back to her
people, Kid. It's beastly hard for a woman
to go back. Think of it! — nearly four
years on our bacon and beans and flour and
dried fruit, and then to go back to her fish
and cariboo. It's not good for her to have
tried our ways, to come to know they're better 'n her people's, and then return to them.
Take care of her, Kid, — why don't you, —
but n , you always fought shy of them, —
and y u never told me why you came to this
country. Be kind to her, and send her back
to the States as soon as you can. But fix it

so as she can come back, — liable to get homesick, you know.

"And the youngster — it's drawn us closer, Kid. I only hope it is a boy. Think of it! — flesh of my flesh, Kid. He mustn't stop in this country. And if it's a girl, why she can't. Sell my furs; they'll fetch at least five thousand, and I've got as much more with the company. And handle my interests with yours. I think that bench claim will show up. See that he gets a good schooling; and Kid, above all, don't let him come back. This country was not made for white men.

"I'm a gone man, Kid. Three or four sleeps at the best. You've got to go on. You must go on! Remember, it's my wife, it's my boy, — O God! I hope it's a boy! You can't stay by me, — and I charge you, a dying man, to pull on."

"Give me three days," pleaded Malemute Kid. "You may change for the better; something may turn up."

"No."

"Just three days."

"You must pull on."

"Two days."

"It's my wife and my boy, Kid. You would not ask it."

"One day."

"No, no! I charge" —

"Only one day. We can shave it through on the grub, and I might knock over a moose."

"No, — all right; one day, but not a minute more. And Kid, don't — don't leave me to face it alone. Just a shot, one pull on the trigger. You understand. Think of it! Think of it! Flesh of my flesh, and I'll never live to see him!

"Send Ruth here. I want to say good-by and tell her that she must think of the boy and not wait till I'm dead. She might refuse to go with you if I didn't. Good-by, old man; good-by.

"Kid! I say — a — sink a hole above the pup, next to the slide. I panned out forty cents on my shovel there.

"And Kid!" he stooped lower to catch the last faint words, the dying man's surrender of his pride. "I'm sorry — for — you know — Carmen."

Leaving the girl crying softly over her man, Malemute Kid slipped into his *parka* and snowshoes, tucked his rifle under his arm, and crept away into the forest. He was no tyro in the stern sorrows of the Northland, but never had he faced so stiff a problem as this. In the abstract, it was a plain, mathematical proposition, — three possible lives as against one doomed one. But now he hesitated. For five years, shoulder to shoulder, on the rivers and trails, in the camps and mines, facing death by field and flood and famine, had they knitted the bonds of their comradeship. So close was the tie, that he had often been conscious of a vague jealousy of Ruth, from the first time she had come between. And now it must be severed by his own hand.

Though he prayed for a moose, just one moose, all game seemed to have deserted the land, and nightfall found the exhausted man crawling into camp, light-handed, heavy-hearted. An uproar from the dogs and shrill cries from Ruth hastened him.

Bursting into the camp, he saw the girl in the midst of the snarling pack, laying about her with an axe. The dogs had broken the iron rule of their masters and were rushing the grub. He joined the issue with his rifle reversed, and the hoary game of natural selection was played out with all the ruthlessness of its primeval environment. Rifle and axe went up and down, hit or missed with monotonous regularity; lithe bodies flashed, with wild eyes and dripping fangs; and man and beast fought for supremacy to the bitterest conclusion. Then the beaten brutes crept to the edge of the firelight, licking their wounds, voicing their misery to the stars.

The whole stock of dried salmon had been devoured, and perhaps five pounds of flour remained to tide them over two hundred miles of wilderness. Ruth returned to her husband, while Malemute Kid cut up the warm body of one of the dogs, the skull of which had been crushed by the axe. Every portion was carefully put away, save the hide and offal, which were cast to his fellows of the moment before.

Morning brought fresh trouble. The animals were turning on each other. Carmen, who still clung to her slender thread of life, was downed by the pack. The lash fell among them unheeded. They cringed and cried under the blows, but refused to scatter till the last wretched bit had disappeared, — bones, hide, hair, everything.

Malemute Kid went about his work, listening to Mason, who was back in Tennessee, delivering tangled discourses and wild exhortations to his brethren of other days.

Taking advantage of neighboring pines, he worked rapidly, and Ruth watched him make a cache similar to those sometimes used by hunters to preserve their meat from the wolverines and dogs. One after the other, he bent the tops of two small pines toward each other and nearly to the ground, making them fast with thongs of moosehide. Then he beat the dogs into submission and harnessed them to two of the sleds, loading the same with everything but the furs which enveloped Mason. These he wrapped and lashed tightly about him, fastening either end of the robes to the bent pines. A single stroke of his hunting-knife would release them and send the body high in the air.

Ruth had received her husband's last wishes and made no struggle. Poor girl, she had learned the lesson of obedience well. From a child, she had bowed, and seen all women bow, to the lords of creation, and it did not seem in the nature of things for woman to resist. The Kid permitted her one outburst of grief, as she kissed her husband, — her own people had no such custom, — then led her to the foremost sled and helped her into her snowshoes. Blindly, instinctively, she took the gee-pole and whip, and "mushed" the dogs out on the trail. Then he returned to Mason, who had fallen into a coma; and long after she was out of sight, crouched by the fire, waiting, hoping, praying for his comrade to die.

It is not pleasant to be alone with painful thoughts in the White Silence. The silence of gloom is merciful, shrouding one as with protection and breathing a thousand intangible sympathies; but the bright White Silence, clear and cold, under steely skies, is pitiless.

An hour passed, — two hours, — but the man would not die. At high noon, the sun, without raising its rim above the southern horizon, threw a suggestion of fire athwart the heavens, then quickly drew it back. Malemute Kid roused and dragged himself to his comrade's side. He cast one glance about him. The White Silence seemed to sneer, and a great fear came upon him. There was a sharp report; Mason swung into his aerial sepulchre; and Malemute Kid lashed the dogs into a wild gallop as he fled across the snow.

THE SON OF THE WOLF

MAN rarely places a proper valuation upon his womankind, at least not until deprived of them. He has no conception of the subtle atmosphere exhaled by the sex feminine so long as he bathes in it; but let it be withdrawn, and an ever-growing void begins to manifest itself in his existence, and he becomes hungry, in a vague sort of way, for a something so indefinite that he cannot characterize it. If his comrades have no more experience than himself, they will shake their heads dubiously and dose him with strong physic. But the hunger will continue and become stronger; he will lose interest in the things of his every-day life and wax morbid; and one day, when the emptiness has become unbearable, a revelation will dawn upon him.

In the Yukon country, when this comes to pass, the man usually provisions a poling-boat, if it be summer, and if winter harnesses his dogs, and heads for the Southland. A few months later, supposing him to be possessed

of a faith in the country, he returns with a
wife to share with him in that faith, and incidentally in his hardships.   This but serves to
show the innate selfishness of man.   It also
brings us to the trouble of " Scruff " Mackenzie, which occurred in the old days, before
the country was stampeded and staked by a
tidal-wave of *che-cha-quas*, and when the
Klondike's only claim to notice was its salmon
fisheries.

Scruff Mackenzie bore the ear-marks of a
frontier birth and a frontier life.   His face
was stamped with twenty-five years of inces-
sant struggle with nature in her wildest moods,
— the last two, the wildest and hardest of all,
having been spent in groping for the gold
which lies in the shadow of the Arctic Circle.
When the yearning sickness came upon him
he was not surprised, for he was a practical
man and had seen other men thus stricken.
But he showed no sign of his malady, save
that he worked harder.   All summer he fought
mosquitoes and washed the sure-thing bars of
the Stuart River for a double grub-stake.
Then he floated a raft of house-logs down the
Yukon to Forty Mile, and put together as
comfortable a cabin as any the camp could

boast of. In fact, it showed such cosy promise that many men elected to be his partner and to come and live with him. But he crushed their aspirations with rough speech, peculiar for its strength and brevity, and bought a double supply of grub from the trading-post.

As has been noted, Scruff Mackenzie was a practical man. If he wanted a thing he usually got it, but in doing so, went no farther out of his way than was necessary. Though a son of toil and hardship, he was averse to a journey of six hundred miles on the ice, a second of two thousand miles on the ocean, and still a third thousand miles or so to his last stamping-grounds, — all in the mere quest of a wife. Life was too short. So he rounded up his dogs, lashed a curious freight to his sled, and faced across the divide whose westward slopes were drained by the head-reaches of the Tanana.

He was a sturdy traveler, and his wolf-dogs could work harder and travel farther on less grub than any other team in the Yukon. Three weeks later he strode into a hunting-camp of the Upper Tanana Sticks. They marveled at his temerity; for they had a bad

name and had been known to kill white men
for as trifling a thing as a sharp axe or a broken
rifle. But he went among them single-handed,
his bearing being a delicious composite of
humility, familiarity, *sang-froid*, and inso-
lence. It required a deft hand and deep
knowledge of the barbaric mind effectually
to handle such diverse weapons ; but he was
a past master in the art, knowing when to
conciliate and when to threaten with Jove-like
wrath.

He first made obeisance to the Chief Thling-
Tinneh, presenting him with a couple of
pounds of black tea and tobacco, and thereby
winning his most cordial regard. Then he
mingled with the men and maidens, and that
night gave a *potlach*. The snow was beaten
down in the form of an oblong, perhaps a
hundred feet in length and quarter as many
across. Down the centre a long fire was
built, while either side was carpeted with
spruce boughs. The lodges were forsaken,
and the fivescore or so members of the tribe
gave tongue to their folk-chants in honor of
their guest.

Scruff Mackenzie's two years had taught
him the not many hundred words of their

vocabulary, and he had likewise conquered
their deep gutturals, their Japanese idioms,
constructions, and honorific and agglutinative
particles. So he made oration after their
manner, satisfying their instinctive poetry-
love with crude flights of eloquence and meta-
phorical contortions. After Thling-Tinneh
and the Shaman had responded in kind, he
made trifling presents to the menfolk, joined
in their singing, and proved an expert in
their fifty-two-stick gambling game.

And they smoked his tobacco and were
pleased. But among the younger men there
was a defiant attitude, a spirit of braggadocio,
easily understood by the raw insinuations of
the toothless squaws and the giggling of the
maidens. They had known few white men,
" Sons of the Wolf," but from those few they
had learned strange lessons.

Nor had Scruff Mackenzie, for all his
seeming carelessness, failed to note these phe-
nomena. In truth, rolled in his sleeping-furs,
he thought it all over, thought seriously, and
emptied many pipes in mapping out a campaign. One maiden only had caught his fancy,
— none other than Zarinska, daughter to the
chief. In features, form, and poise, answer-

ing more nearly to the white man's type of beauty, she was almost an anomaly among her tribal sisters. He would possess her, make her his wife, and name her — ah, he would name her Gertrude! Having thus decided, he rolled over on his side and dropped off to sleep, a true son of his all-conquering race.

It was slow work and a stiff game; but Scruff Mackenzie manœuvred cunningly, with an unconcern which served to puzzle the Sticks. He took great care to impress the men that he was a sure shot and a mighty hunter, and the camp rang with his plaudits when he brought down a moose at six hundred yards. Of a night he visited in Chief Thling-Tinneh's lodge of moose and cariboo skins, talking big and dispensing tobacco with a lavish hand. Nor did he fail to likewise honor the Shaman; for he realized the medicine-man's influence with his people, and was anxious to make of him an ally. But that worthy was high and mighty, refused to be propitiated, and was unerringly marked down as a prospective enemy.

Though no opening presented for an interview with Zarinska, Mackenzie stole many a glance to her, giving fair warning of his intent. And well she knew, yet coquettishly surrounded herself with a ring of women whenever the men were away and he had a chance. But he was in no hurry; besides, he knew she could not help but think of him, and a few days of such thought would only better his suit.

At last, one night, when he deemed the time to be ripe, he abruptly left the chief's smoky dwelling and hastened to a neighboring lodge. As usual, she sat with squaws and maidens about her, all engaged in sewing moccasins and beadwork. They laughed at his entrance, and badinage, which linked Zarinska to him, ran high. But one after the other they were unceremoniously bundled into the outer snow, whence they hurried to spread the tale through all the camp.

His cause was well pleaded, in her tongue, for she did not know his, and at the end of two hours he rose to go.

"So Zarinska will come to the White Man's lodge? Good! I go now to have talk with thy father, for he may not be so minded. And I will give him many tokens; but he must not ask too much. If he say no? Good!

Zarinska shall yet come to the White Man's lodge."

He had already lifted the skin flap to depart, when a low exclamation brought him back to the girl's side. She brought herself to her knees on the bearskin mat, her face aglow with true Eve-light, and shyly unbuckled his heavy belt. He looked down, perplexed, suspicious, his ears alert for the slightest sound without. But her next move disarmed his doubt, and he smiled with pleasure. She took from her sewing - bag a moosehide sheath, brave with bright beadwork, fantastically designed. She drew his great hunting-knife, gazed reverently along the keen edge, half tempted to try it with her thumb, and shot it into place in its new home. Then she slipped the sheath along the belt to its customary resting-place, just above the hip.

For all the world, it was like a scene of olden time, — a lady and her knight. Mackenzie drew her up full height and swept her red lips with his mustache, — the, to her, foreign caress of the Wolf. It was a meeting of the stone age and the steel.

There was a thrill of excitement in the air

It was like a scene of olden time———
a lady and her knight.

as Scruff Mackenzie, a bulky bundle under his arm, threw open the flap of Thling-Tinneh's tent. Children were running about in the open, dragging dry wood to the scene of the *potlach*, a babble of women's voices was growing in intensity, the young men were consulting in sullen groups, while from the Shaman's lodge rose the eerie sounds of an incantation.

The chief was alone with his blear-eyed wife, but a glance sufficed to tell Mackenzie that the news was already old. So he plunged at once into the business, shifting the beaded sheath prominently to the fore as advertisement of the betrothal.

" O Thling-Tinneh, mighty chief of the Sticks and the land of the Tanana, ruler of the salmon and the bear, the moose and the cariboo! The White Man is before thee with a great purpose. Many moons has his lodge been empty, and he is lonely. And his heart has eaten itself in silence, and grown hungry for a woman to sit beside him in his lodge, to meet him from the hunt with warm fire and good food. He has heard strange things, the patter of baby moccasins and the sound of children's voices. And one night a vision came upon him, and he beheld the Raven, who is thy father, the great Raven, who is the father of all the Sticks. And the Raven spake to the lonely White Man, saying: 'Bind thou thy moccasins upon thee, and gird thy snowshoes on, and lash thy sled with food for many sleeps and fine tokens for the Chief Thling-Tinneh. For thou shalt turn thy face to where the midspring sun is wont to sink below the land, and journey to this great chief's hunting-grounds. There thou shalt make big presents, and Thling-Tinneh, who is my son, shall become to thee as a father. In his lodge there is a maiden into whom I breathed the breath of life for thee. This maiden shalt thou take to wife.'

"O Chief, thus spake the great Raven; thus do I lay many presents at thy feet; thus am I come to take thy daughter!"

The old man drew his furs about him with crude consciousness of royalty, but delayed reply while a youngster crept in, delivered a quick message to appear before the council, and was gone.

"O White Man, whom we have named Moose-Killer, also known as the Wolf, and the Son of the Wolf! We know thou comest of

a mighty race; we are proud to have thee
our *potlach*-guest; but the king-salmon does
not mate with the dog-salmon, nor the Raven
with the Wolf."

"Not so!" cried Mackenzie. "The daughters of the Raven have I met in the camps
of the Wolf,— the squaw of Mortimer, the
squaw of Tregidgo, the squaw of Barnaby,
who came two ice-runs back, and I have heard
of other squaws, though my eyes beheld them
not."

"Son, your words are true; but it were
evil mating, like the water with the sand, like
the snowflake with the sun. But met you
one Mason and his squaw? No? He came
ten ice-runs ago,— the first of all the Wolves.
And with him there was a mighty man,
straight as a willow-shoot, and tall; strong as
the bald-faced grizzly, with a heart like the
full summer moon; his"—

"Oh!" interrupted Mackenzie, recogniz-
ing the well-known Northland figure,—
"Malemute Kid!"

"The same,— a mighty man. But saw
you aught of the squaw? She was full sister to Zarinska."

"Nay, Chief; but I have heard. Mason

— far, far to the north, a spruce-tree, heavy with years, crushed out his life beneath. But his love was great, and he had much gold. With this, and her boy, she journeyed countless sleeps toward the winter's noonday sun, and there she yet lives, — no biting frost, no snow, no summer's midnight sun, no winter's noonday night."

A second messenger interrupted with imperative summons from the council. As Mackenzie threw him into the snow, he caught a glimpse of the swaying forms before the council-fire, heard the deep basses of the men in rhythmic chant, and knew the Shaman was fanning the anger of his people. Time pressed. He turned upon the chief.

"Come! I wish thy child. And now. See! here are tobacco, tea, many cups of sugar, warm blankets, handkerchiefs, both good and large; and here, a true rifle, with many bullets and much powder."

"Nay," replied the old man, struggling against the great wealth spread before him. "Even now are my people come together. They will not have this marriage."

"But thou art chief."

"Yet do my young men rage because the

Wolves have taken their maidens so that they may not marry."

"Listen, O Thling-Tinneh! Ere the night has passed into the day, the Wolf shall face his dogs to the Mountains of the East and fare forth to the Country of the Yukon. And Zarinska shall break trail for his dogs."

"And ere the night has gained its middle, my young men may fling to the dogs the flesh of the Wolf, and his bones be scattered in the snow till the springtime lay them bare."

It was threat and counter-threat. Mackenzie's bronzed face flushed darkly. He raised his voice. The old squaw, who till now had sat an impassive spectator, made to creep by him for the door. The song of the men broke suddenly, and there was a hubbub of many voices as he whirled the old woman roughly to her couch of skins.

"Again I cry — listen, O Thling-Tinneh! The Wolf dies with teeth fast-locked, and with him there shall sleep ten of thy strongest men, — men who are needed, for the hunting is but begun, and the fishing is not many moons away. And again, of what profit should I die? I know the custom of thy people; thy share of my wealth shall be very small. Grant me thy child, and it shall all be thine. And yet again, my brothers will come, and they are many, and their maws are never filled; and the daughters of the Raven shall bear children in the lodges of the Wolf. My people are greater than thy people. It is destiny. Grant, and all this wealth is thine."

Moccasins were crunching the snow without. Mackenzie threw his rifle to cock, and loosened the twin Colts in his belt.

"Grant, O Chief!"

"And yet will my people say no."

"Grant, and the wealth is thine. Then shall I deal with thy people after."

"The Wolf will have it so. I will take his tokens, — but I would warn him."

Mackenzie passed over the goods, taking care to clog the rifle's ejector, and capping the bargain with a kaleidoscopic silk kerchief. The Shaman and half a dozen young braves entered, but he shouldered boldly among them and passed out.

"Pack!" was his laconic greeting to Zarinska as he passed her lodge and hurried to harness his dogs. A few minutes later he swept into the council at the head of the team, the woman by his side. He took his place at the upper end of the oblong, by the side of the chief. To his left, a step to the rear, he stationed Zarinska, — her proper place. Besides, the time was ripe for mischief, and there was need to guard his back.

On either side, the men crouched to the fire, their voices lifted in a folk-chant out of the forgotten past. Full of strange; halting cadences and haunting recurrences, it was not beautiful. " Fearful " may inadequately express it. At the lower end, under the eye of the Shaman, danced half a score of women. Stern were his reproofs to those who did not wholly abandon themselves to the ecstasy of the rite. Half hidden in their heavy masses of raven hair, all disheveled and falling to their waists, they slowly swayed to and fro, their forms rippling to an ever-changing rhythm.

It was a weird scene ; an anachronism. To the south, the nineteenth century was reeling off the few years of its last decade ; here flourished man primeval, a shade removed from the prehistoric cave-dweller, a forgotten fragment of the Elder World. The tawny wolf-dogs sat between their skin-clad masters or fought for room, the firelight cast

backward from their red eyes and slavered
fangs. The woods, in ghostly shroud, slept
on unheeding. The White Silence, for the
moment driven to the rimming forest, seemed
ever crushing inward ; the stars danced with
great leaps, as is their wont in the time of
the Great Cold ; while the Spirits of the Pole
trailed their robes of glory athwart the heavens.

Scruff Mackenzie dimly realized the wild
grandeur of the setting as his eyes ranged
down the fur-fringed sides in quest of missing faces. They rested for a moment on a
newborn babe, suckling at its mother's naked
breast. It was forty below, — seventy and
odd degrees of frost. He thought of the tender women of his own race, and smiled grimly.
Yet from the loins of some such tender woman
had he sprung with a kingly inheritance, —
an inheritance which gave to him and his dom-
inance over the land and sea, over the animals and the peoples of all the zones. Single-
handed against fivescore, girt by the Arctic
winter, far from his own, he felt the prompt-
ing of his heritage, the desire to possess,
the wild danger-love, the thrill of battle, the
power to conquer or to die.

The singing and the dancing ceased, and the Shaman flared up in rude eloquence. Through the sinuosities of their vast mythology, he worked cunningly upon the credulity of his people. The case was strong. Opposing the creative principles as embodied in the Crow and the Raven, he stigmatized Mackenzie as the Wolf, the fighting and the destructive principle. Not only was the combat of these forces spiritual, but men fought, each to his totem. They were the children of Jelchs, the Raven, the Promethean firebringer; Mackenzie was the child of the Wolf, or, in other words, the Devil. For them to bring a truce to this perpetual warfare, to marry their daughters to the archenemy, were treason and blasphemy of the highest order. No phrase was harsh, nor figure vile, enough in branding Mackenzie as a sneaking interloper and emissary of Satan. There was a subdued, savage roar in the deep chests of his listeners as he took the swing of his peroration.

"Ay, my brothers, Jelchs is all-powerful! Did he not bring heaven-born fire that we might be warm? Did he not draw the sun, moon, and stars from their holes that we might see? Did he not teach us that we might fight the Spirits of Famine and of Frost? But now Jelchs is angry with his children, and they are grown to a handful, and he will not help. For they have forgotten him, and done evil things, and trod bad trails, and taken his enemies into their lodges to sit by their fires. And the Raven is sorrowful at the wickedness of his children; but when they shall rise up and show they have come back, he will come out of the darkness to aid them. O brothers! the Fire-Bringer has whispered messages to thy Shaman; the same shall ye hear. Let the young men take the young women to their lodges; let them fly at the throat of the Wolf; let them be undying in their enmity! Then shall their women become fruitful, and they shall multiply into a mighty people! And the Raven shall lead great tribes of their fathers and their fathers' fathers from out of the North; and they shall beat back the Wolves till they are as last year's camp-fires; and they shall again come to rule over all the land! 'T is the message of Jelchs, the Raven."

This foreshadowing of the Messiah's coming brought a hoarse howl from the Sticks

as they leaped to their feet. Mackenzie
slipped the thumbs of his mittens, and waited.
There was a clamor for the Fox, not to be
stilled till one of the young men stepped forward to speak.

" Brothers ! The Shaman has spoken
wisely. The Wolves have taken our women,
and our men are childless. We are grown
to a handful. The Wolves have taken our
warm furs, and given for them evil spirits
which dwell in bottles, and clothes which
come not from the beaver or the lynx, but
are made from the grass. And they are not
warm, and our men die of strange sicknesses.
I, the Fox, have taken no woman to wife ;
and why? Twice have the maidens which
pleased me gone to the camps of the Wolf.
Even now have I laid by skins of the beaver,
of the moose, of the cariboo, that I might win
favor in the eyes of Thling-Tinneh, that I
might marry Zarinska, his daughter. Even
now are her snowshoes bound to her feet,
ready to break trail for the dogs of the Wolf.
Nor do I speak for myself alone. As I have
done, so has the Bear. He, too, had fain
been the father of her children, and many
skins has he cured thereto. I speak for all

the young men who know not wives. The Wolves are ever hungry. Always do they take the choice meat at the killing. To the Ravens are left the leavings.

"There is Gugkla!" he cried, brutally pointing out one of the women, who was a cripple. "Her legs are bent like the ribs of a birch canoe. She cannot gather wood nor carry the meat of the hunters. Did the Wolves choose her?"

"Ai! ai!" vociferated his tribesmen.

"There is Moyri, whose eyes are crossed by the Evil Spirit. Even the babes are affrighted when they gaze upon her, and it is said the bald-face gives her the trail. Was she chosen?"

Again the cruel applause rang out.

"And there sits Pischet. She does not hearken to my words. Never has she heard the cry of the chit-chat, the voice of her husband, the babble of her child. She lives in the White Silence. Cared the Wolves aught for her? No! Theirs is the choice of the kill; ours is the leavings.

"Brothers, it shall not be! No more shall the Wolves slink among our camp-fires. The time is come."

A great streamer of fire, the aurora bore-alis, purple, green, and yellow, shot across the zenith, bridging horizon to horizon. With head thrown back and arms extended, he swayed to his climax.

" Behold !   The spirits of our fathers have arisen and great deeds are afoot this night ! "

He stepped back, and another young man somewhat diffidently came forward, pushed on by his comrades. He towered a full head above them, his broad chest defiantly bared to the frost. He swung tentatively from one foot to the other. Words halted upon his tongue, and he was ill at ease. His face was horrible to look upon, for it had at one time been half torn away by some ter-rific blow. At last he struck his breast with his clenched fist, drawing sound as from a drum, and his voice rumbled forth as the surf from an ocean cavern.

" I am the Bear, — the Silver-Tip and the Son of the Silver-Tip ! When my voice was yet as a girl's, I slew the lynx, the moose, and the cariboo ; when it whistled like the wol-verines from under a cache, I crossed the Mountains of the South and slew three of the White Rivers ; when it became as the roar of the Chinook, I met the bald-faced grizzly, but gave no trail."

At this he paused, his hand significantly sweeping across his hideous scars.

"I am not as the Fox. My tongue is frozen like the river. I cannot make great talk. My words are few. The Fox says great deeds are afoot this night. Good! Talk flows from his tongue like the freshets of the spring, but he is chary of deeds. This night shall I do battle with the Wolf. I shall slay him, and Zarinska shall sit by my fire. The Bear has spoken."

Though pandemonium raged about him, Scruff Mackenzie held his ground. Aware how useless was the rifle at close quarters, he slipped both holsters to the fore, ready for action, and drew his mittens till his hands were barely shielded by the elbow gauntlets. He knew there was no hope in attack *en masse*, but true to his boast, was prepared to die with teeth fast-locked. But the Bear restrained his comrades, beating back the more impetuous with his terrible fist. As the tumult began to die away, Mackenzie shot a glance in the direction of Zarinska. It was a superb picture. She was leaning forward

on her snowshoes, lips apart and nostrils
quivering, like a tigress about to spring.
Her great black eyes were fixed upon her
tribesmen, in fear and in defiance. So ex-
treme the tension, she had forgotten to
breathe. With one hand pressed spasmod-
ically against her breast and the other as
tightly gripped about the dogwhip, she was
as turned to stone. Even as he looked, relief
came to her. Her muscles loosened; with a
heavy sigh she settled back, giving him a
look of more than love.

Thling-Tinneh was trying to speak, but his
people drowned his voice. Then Mackenzie
strode forward. The Fox opened mouth to a
piercing yell, but so savagely did Mackenzie
whirl upon him that he shrank back, his
larynx all a-gurgle with suppressed sound.
His discomfiture was greeted with roars of
laughter, and served to soothe his fellows to
a listening mood.

"Brothers! The White Man, whom ye
have chosen to call the Wolf, came among
you with fair words. He was not like the
Innuit; he spoke not lies. He came as a
friend, as one who would be a brother. But
your men have had their say, and the time

for soft words is past. First, I will tell you
that the Shaman has an evil tongue and is a
false prophet, that the messages he spake are
not those of the Fire-Bringer. His ears are
locked to the voice of the Raven, and out of
his own head he weaves cunning fancies, and
he has made fools of you. He has no power.
When the dogs were killed and eaten, and
your stomachs were heavy with untanned
hide and strips of moccasins ; when the old
men died, and the old women died, and the
babes at the dry dugs of the mothers died ;
when the land was dark, and ye perished as
do the salmon in the fall ; ay, when the
famine was upon you, did the Shaman bring
reward to your hunters ? did the Shaman put
meat in your bellies ? Again I say, the Shaman is without power. Thus! I spit upon his
face ! ''

Though taken aback by the sacrilege, there
was no uproar. Some of the women were
even frightened, but among the men there
was an uplifting, as though in preparation or
anticipation of the miracle. All eyes were
turned upon the two central figures. The
priest realized the crucial moment, felt his
power tottering, opened his mouth in denun-

ciation, but fled backward before the trucu-
lent advance, upraised fist, and flashing eyes
of Mackenzie. He sneered and resumed.

"Was I stricken dead? Did the lightning
burn me? Did the stars fall from the sky
and crush me? Pish! I have done with the
dog. Now will I tell you of my people, who
are the mightiest of all the peoples, who rule
in all the lands. At first we hunt as I hunt,
alone. After that we hunt in packs; and at
last, like the cariboo-run, we sweep across all
the land. Those whom we take into our
lodges live; those who will not come die.
Zarinska is a comely maiden, full and strong,
fit to become the mother of Wolves. Though
I die, such shall she become; for my brothers
are many, and they will follow the scent of
my dogs. Listen to the Law of the Wolf:
*Whoso taketh the life of one Wolf, the for-
feit shall ten of his people pay.* In many
lands has the price been paid; in many lands
shall it yet be paid.

"Now will I deal with the Fox and the
Bear. It seems they have cast eyes upon the
maiden. So? Behold, I have bought her!
Thling-Tinneh leans upon the rifle; the goods
of purchase are by his fire. Yet will I be

fair to the young men. To the Fox, whose tongue is dry with many words, will I give of tobacco five long plugs. Thus will his mouth be wetted that he may make much noise in the council. But to the Bear, of whom I am well proud, will I give of blankets two; of flour, twenty cups; of tobacco, double that of the Fox; and if he fare with me over the Mountains of the East, then will I give him a rifle, mate to Thling-Tinneh's. If not? Good! The Wolf is weary of speech. Yet once again will he say the Law: *Whoso taketh the life of one Wolf, the forfeit shall ten of his people pay.*'

Mackenzie smiled as he stepped back to his old position, but at heart he was full of trouble. The night was yet dark. The girl came to his side, and he listened closely as she told of the Bear's battle-tricks with the knife.

The decision was for war. In a trice, scores of moccasins were widening the space of beaten snow by the fire. There was much chatter about the seeming defeat of the Shaman; some averred he had but withheld his power, while others conned past events and agreed with the Wolf. The Bear came to the centre of the battle-ground, a long naked hunting-knife of Russian make in his hand. The Fox called attention to Mackenzie's revolvers; so he stripped his belt, buckling it about Zarinska, into whose hands he also intrusted his rifle. She shook her head that she could not shoot, — small chance had a woman to handle such precious things.

"Then, if danger come by my back, cry aloud, 'My husband!' No; thus, 'My husband!'"

He laughed as she repeated it, pinched her cheek, and reëntered the circle. Not only in reach and stature had the Bear the advantage of him, but his blade was longer by a good two inches. Scruff Mackenzie had looked into the eyes of men before, and he knew it was a man who stood against him; yet he quickened to the glint of light on the steel, to the dominant pulse of his race.

Time and again he was forced to the edge of the fire or the deep snow, and time and again, with the foot tactics of the pugilist, he worked back to the centre. Not a voice was lifted in encouragement, while his antagonist was heartened with applause, suggestions, and warnings. But his teeth only

shut the tighter as the knives clashed together, and he thrust or eluded with a cool-
ness born of conscious strength. At first he
felt compassion for his enemy; but this fled
before the primal instinct of life, which in
turn gave way to the lust of slaughter. The
ten thousand years of culture fell from him,
and he was a cave-dweller, doing battle for
his female.

Twice he pricked the Bear, getting away
unscathed; but the third time caught, and
to save himself, free hands closed on fighting
hands, and they came together. Then did
he realize the tremendous strength of his op-
ponent. His muscles were knotted in painful lumps, and cords and tendons threatened
to snap with the strain; yet nearer and
nearer came the Russian steel. He tried to
break away, but only weakened himself. The
fur-clad circle closed in, certain of and anxious to see the final stroke. But with wres-
tler's trick, swinging partly to the side, he
struck at his adversary with his head. Involuntarily the Bear leaned back, disturbing his
centre of gravity. Simultaneous with this,
Mackenzie tripped properly and threw his
whole weight forward, hurling him clear

through the circle into the deep snow. The Bear floundered out and came back full tilt.

" O my husband!" Zarinska's voice rang out, vibrant with danger.

To the twang of a bow-string, Mackenzie swept low to the ground, and a bone-barbed arrow passed over him into the breast of the Bear, whose momentum carried him over his crouching foe. The next instant Mackenzie was up and about. The Bear lay motionless, but across the fire was the Shaman, drawing a second arrow.

Mackenzie's knife leaped short in the air. He caught the heavy blade by the point. There was a flash of light as it spanned the fire. Then the Shaman, the hilt alone appearing without his throat, swayed a moment and pitched forward into the glowing embers.

Click! click! — the Fox had possessed himself of Thling-Tinneh's rifle and was vainly trying to throw a shell into place. But he dropped it at the sound of Mackenzie's laughter.

" So the Fox has not learned the way of the plaything? He is yet a woman. Come! Bring it, that I may show thee!"

The Fox hesitated.

" Come, I say ! "

He slouched forward like a beaten cur.

" Thus, and thus ; so the thing is done."
A shell flew into place and the trigger was at
cock as Mackenzie brought it to shoulder.

" The Fox has said great deeds were afoot
this night, and he spoke true. There have
been great deeds, yet least among them were
those of the Fox. Is he still intent to take
Zarinska to his lodge ? Is he minded to tread
the trail already broken by the Shaman and
the Bear ? No ? Good ! "

Mackenzie turned contemptuously and
drew his knife from the priest's throat.

" Are any of the young men so minded ?
If so, the Wolf will take them by two and
three till none are left. No ? Good ! Thling-
Tinneh, I now give thee this rifle a second
time. If in the days to come thou shouldst
journey to the Country of the Yukon, know
thou that there shall always be a place and
much food by the fire of the Wolf. The
night is now passing into the day. I go, but
I may come again. And for the last time,
remember the Law of the Wolf ! "

He was supernatural in their sight as he

rejoined Zarinska. She took her place at the head of the team, and the dogs swung into motion. A few moments later they were swallowed up by the ghostly forest. Till now Mackenzie had waited; he slipped into his snowshoes to follow.

"Has the Wolf forgotten the five long plugs?"

Mackenzie turned upon the Fox angrily; then the humor of it struck him.

"I will give thee one short plug."

"As the Wolf sees fit," meekly responded the Fox, stretching out his hand.

THE MEN OF FORTY-MILE

When Big Jim Belden ventured the apparently innocuous proposition that mush-ice was "rather pecooliar," he little dreamed of what it would lead to. Neither did Lon McFane, when he affirmed that anchor-ice was even more so; nor did Bettles, as he instantly disagreed, declaring the very existence of such a form to be a bugaboo.

"An' ye 'd be tellin' me this," cried Lon, "after the years ye 've spint in the land! An' we atin' out the same pot this many 's the day!"

"But the thing 's agin reason," insisted Bettles. "Look you, water 's warmer than ice" —

"An' little the difference, once ye break through."

"Still it 's warmer, because it ain't froze. An' you say it freezes on the bottom?"

"Only the anchor-ice, David, only the anchor-ice. An' have ye niver drifted along, the water clear as glass, whin suddin, belike

a cloud over the sun, the mushy ice comes
bubblin' up an' up, till from bank to bank
an' bind to bind it 's drapin' the river like a
first snowfall ? "

" Unh hunh ! more 'n once when I took
a doze at the steering-oar. But it allus come
out the nighest side-channel, an' not bubblin'
up an' up."

" But with niver a wink at the helm ? "

" No ; nor you. It 's agin reason. I 'll
leave it to any man ! "

Bettles appealed to the circle about the
stove, but the fight was on between himself
and Lon McFane.

" Reason or no reason, it 's the truth I 'm
tellin' ye. Last fall, a year gone, 't was
Sitka Charley and meself saw the sight, drop-
pin' down the riffle ye 'll remember below
Fort Reliance. An' regular fall weather it
was, — the glint o' the sun on the golden
larch an' the quakin' aspens ; an' the glister
of light on ivery ripple ; an' beyand, the winter an' the blue haze of the North comin'
down hand in hand. It 's well ye know the
same, with a fringe to the river an' the ice
formin' thick in the eddies, — an' a snap
an' sparkle to the air, an' ye a-feelin' it

through all yer blood, a-takin' new lease of
life with ivery suck of it. 'T is then, me boy,
the world grows small an' the wandther-lust
lays ye by the heels.

"But it's meself as wandthers. As I was
sayin', we a-paddlin', with niver a sign of ice,
barrin' that by the eddies, when the Injin
lifts his paddle an' sings out, ' Lon McFane!
Look ye below! So have I heard, but niver
thought to see!' As ye know, Sitka Charley,
like meself, niver drew first breath in the
land; so the sight was new. Then we drifted,
with a head over ayther side, peerin' down
through the sparkly water. For the world
like the days I spint with the pearlers,
watchin' the coral banks a-growin' the same
as so many gardens under the sea. There it
was, the anchor-ice, clingin' an' clusterin' to
ivery rock, after the manner of the white
coral.

"But the best of the sight was to come.
Just after clearin' the tail of the riffle, the
water turns quick the color of milk, an' the
top of it in wee circles, as when the graylin'
rise in the spring or there's a splatter of wet
from the sky. 'T was the anchor-ice comin'
up. To the right, to the lift, as far as iver

a man cud see, the water was covered with
the same. An' like so much porridge it was,
slickin' along the bark of the canoe, stickin'
like glue to the paddles. It's many's the
time I shot the selfsame riffle before, and it's
many's the time after, but niver a wink of
the same have I seen. 'T was the sight of a
lifetime."

"Do tell!" dryly commented Bettles. "D'
ye think I'd b'lieve such a yarn? I'd ruther
say the glister of light'd gone to your eyes,
and the snap of the air to your tongue."

"'T was me own eyes that beheld it, an' if
Sitka Charley was here, he'd be the lad to
back me."

"But facts is facts, an' they ain't no gittin'
round 'em. It ain't in the nature of things
for the water furtherest away from the air to
freeze first."

"But me own eyes" —

"Don't git het up over it," admonished Bettles, as the quick Celtic anger began to mount.

"Then yer not after belavin' me?"

"Sence you're so blamed forehanded about
it, no; I'd b'lieve nature first, and facts."

"Is it the lie ye'd be givin' me?" threatened Lon. "Ye'd better be askin' that Siwash

wife of yours. I 'll lave it to her, for the truth I spake."

Bettles flared up in sudden wrath. The Irishman had unwittingly wounded him; for his wife was the half-breed daughter of a Russian fur-trader, married to him in the Greek Mission of Nulato, a thousand miles or so down the Yukon, thus being of much higher caste than the common Siwash, or native, wife. It was a mere Northland nuance, which none but the Northland adventurer may understand.

"I reckon you kin take it that way," was his deliberate affirmation.

The next instant Lon McFane had stretched him on the floor, the circle was broken up, and half a dozen men had stepped between.

Bettles came to his feet, wiping the blood from his mouth. "It hain't new, this takin' and payin' of blows, and don't you never think but that this will be squared."

"An' niver in me life did I take the lie from mortal man," was the retort courteous. "An' it 's an avil day I 'll not be to hand, waitin' an' willin' to help ye lift yer debts, barrin' no manner of way."

"Still got that 38–55 ? "

Lon nodded.

"But you'd better git a more likely calibre. Mine'll rip holes through you the size of walnuts."

"Niver fear; it's me own slugs smell their way with soft noses, an' they'll spread like flapjacks against the coming out beyand. An' when'll I have the pleasure of waitin' on ye? The water-hole's a strikin' locality."

"'T ain't bad. Jest be there in an hour, and you won't set long on my coming."

Both men mittened and left the Post, their ears closed to the remonstrances of their comrades. It was such a little thing; yet with such men, little things, nourished by quick tempers and stubborn natures, soon blossomed into big things. Besides, the art of burning to bed-rock still lay in the womb of the future, and the men of Forty-Mile, shut in by the long Arctic winter, grew high-stomached with over-eating and enforced idleness, and became as irritable as do the bees in the fall of the year when the hives are overstocked with honey.

There was no law in the land. The Mounted Police was also a thing of the future. Each man measured an offense and meted out the punishment in as much as it affected himself. Rarely had combined action been necessary, and never in all the dreary history of the camp had the eighth article of the Decalogue been violated.

Big Jim Belden called an impromptu meeting. Scruff Mackenzie was placed as temporary chairman, and a messenger dispatched to solicit Father Roubeau's good offices. Their position was paradoxical, and they knew it. By the right of might could they interfere to prevent the duel; yet such action, while in direct line with their wishes, went counter to their opinions. While their rough-hewn, obsolete ethics recognized the individual prerogative of wiping out blow with blow, they could not bear to think of two good comrades, such as Bettles and McFane, meeting in deadly battle. Deeming the man who would not fight on provocation a dastard, when brought to the test it seemed wrong that he should fight.

But a scurry of moccasins and loud cries, rounded off with a pistol-shot, interrupted the discussion. Then the storm-doors opened and Malemute Kid entered, a smoking Colt's in his hand and a merry light in his eye.

"I got him." He replaced the empty shell, and added, "Your dog, Scruff."

"Yellow Fang?" Mackenzie asked.

"No; the lop-eared one."

"The devil! Nothing the matter with him."

"Come out and take a look."

"That's all right, after all. Guess he's got 'em, too. Yellow Fang came back this morning and took a chunk out of him, and came near to making a widower of me. Made a rush for Zarinska, but she whisked her skirts in his face and escaped with the loss of the same and a good roll in the snow. Then he took to the woods again. Hope he don't come back. Lost any yourself?"

"One — the best one of the pack — Shookum. Started amuck this morning, but did n't get very far. Ran foul of Sitka Charley's team, and they scattered him all over the street. And now two of them are loose and raging mad; so you see he got his work in. The dog census will be small in the spring if we don't do something."

"And the man census, too."

"How 's that? Whose in trouble now?"

"Oh, Bettles and Lon McFane had an ar-

gument, and they 'll be down by the water-
hole in a few minutes to settle it."

The incident was repeated for his benefit,
and Malemute Kid, accustomed to an obedience which his fellow men never failed to ren-
der, took charge of the affair.   His quickly
formulated plan was explained, and they promised to follow his lead implicitly.

" So you see," he concluded, " we do not
actually take away their privilege of fighting ;
and yet I don't believe they 'll fight when
they see the beauty of the scheme.   Life 's a
game, and men the gamblers.   They 'll stake
their whole pile on the one chance in a thousand.   Take away that one chance, and —
they won't play."

He turned to the man in charge of the
Post.   " Storekeeper, weigh out three fath-
oms of your best half-inch manila."

" We 'll establish a precedent which will
last the men of Forty-Mile to the end of
time," he prophesied.   Then he coiled the
rope about his arm and led his followers out
of doors, just in time to meet the principals.

" What danged right 'd he to fetch my
wife in ?" thundered Bettles to the soothing
overtures of a friend.   " 'T wa'n't called

for," he concluded decisively. " 'T wa'n't called for," he reiterated again and again, pacing up and down and waiting for Lon McFane.

And Lon McFane — his face was hot and tongue rapid as he flaunted insurrection in the face of the Church. " Then, father," he cried, " it 's with an aisy heart I 'll roll in me flamy blankets, the broad of me back on a bed of coals. Niver shall it be said Lon McFane took a lie 'twixt the teeth without iver liftin' a hand! An' I 'll not ask a blessin'. The years have been wild, but it 's the heart was in the right place."

" But it 's not the heart, Lon," interposed Father Roubeau; " it 's pride that bids you forth to slay your fellow man."

" Yer Frinch," Lon replied. And then, turning to leave him, " An' will ye say a mass if the luck is against me? "

But the priest smiled, thrust his moccasined feet to the fore, and went out upon the white breast of the silent river. A packed trail, the width of a sixteen-inch sled, led out to the water-hole. On either side lay the deep, soft snow. The men trod in single file, without conversation; and the black-stoled priest in

their midst gave to the function the solemn
aspect of a funeral. It was a warm winter's
day for Forty-Mile, — a day in which the sky,
filled with heaviness, drew closer to the earth,
and the mercury sought the unwonted level
of twenty below. But there was no cheer in
the warmth. There was little air in the upper
strata, and the clouds hung motionless, giving
sullen promise of an early snowfall. And the
earth, unresponsive, made no preparation,
content in its hibernation.

When the water-hole was reached, Bettles,
having evidently reviewed the quarrel during
the silent walk, burst out in a final "'T wa'n't
called for," while Lon McFane kept grim
silence. Indignation so choked him that he
could not speak.

Yet deep down, whenever their own wrongs
were not uppermost, both men wondered at
their comrades. They had expected opposi-
tion, and this tacit acquiescence hurt them.
It seemed more was due them from the men
they had been so close with, and they felt a
vague sense of wrong, rebelling at the thought
of so many of their brothers coming out, as
on a gala occasion, without one word of protest, to see them shoot each other down. It

appeared their worth had diminished in the eyes of the community. The proceedings puzzled them.

"Back to back, David. An' will it be fifty paces to the man, or double the quantity?"

"Fifty," was the sanguinary reply, grunted out, yet sharply cut.

But the new manila, not prominently displayed but casually coiled about Malemute Kid's arm, caught the quick eye of the Irishman and thrilled him with a suspicious fear.

"An' what are ye doin' with the rope?"

"Hurry up!" Malemute Kid glanced at his watch. "I've a batch of bread in the cabin, and I don't want it to fall. Besides, my feet are getting cold."

The rest of the men manifested their impatience in various suggestive ways.

"But the rope, Kid? It's bran' new, an' sure yer bread's not that heavy it needs raisin' with the like of that?"

Bettles by this time had faced around. Father Roubeau, the humor of the situation just dawning on him, hid a smile behind his mittened hand.

"No, Lon; this rope was made for a man."

Malemute Kid could be very impressive on occasion.

"What man?" Bettles was becoming aware of a personal interest.

"The other man."

"An' which is the one ye 'd mane by that?"

"Listen, Lon, — and you, too, Bettles! We 've been talking this little trouble of yours over, and we 've come to one conclusion. We know we have no right to stop your fighting" —

"True for ye, me lad!"

"And we 're not going to. But this much we can do, and shall do, — make this the only duel in the history of Forty-Mile, set an example for every *che-cha-qua* that comes up or down the Yukon. The man who escapes killing shall be hanged to the nearest tree. Now, go ahead!"

Lon smiled dubiously, then his face lighted up. "Pace her off, David, — fifty paces, wheel, an' niver a cease firin' till a lad 's down for good. 'T is their hearts 'll niver let them do the deed, an' it 's well ye should know it for a true Yankee bluff."

He started off with a pleased grin on his face, but Malemute Kid halted him.

" Lon ! It 's a long while since you first knew me ? "

" Many 's the day."

" And you, Bettles ? "

" Five year next June high water."

" And have you once, in all that time, known me to break my word ? Or heard of me breaking it ? "

Both men shook their heads, striving to fathom what lay beyond.

" Well, then, what do you think of a promise made by me ? "

" As good as your bond," from Bettles.

" The thing to safely sling yer hopes of heaven by," promptly indorsed Lon McFane.

" Listen ! I, Malemute Kid, give you my word — and you know what that means — that the man who is not shot stretches rope within ten minutes after the shooting." He stepped back as Pilate might have done after washing his hands.

A pause and a silence came over the men of Forty-Mile. The sky drew still closer, sending down a crystal flight of frost, — little geometric designs, perfect, evanescent as a breath, yet destined to exist till the returning sun had covered half its northern journey.

Both men had led forlorn hopes in their time, — led, with a curse or a jest on their tongues, and in their souls an unswerving faith in the God of Chance. But that merciful deity had been shut out from the present deal. They studied the face of Malemute Kid, but they studied as one might the Sphinx. As the quiet minutes passed, a feeling that speech was incumbent on them began to grow. At last the howl of a wolf-dog cracked the silence from the direction of Forty-Mile. The weird sound swelled with all the pathos of a breaking heart, then died away in a long-drawn sob.

"Well I be danged!" Bettles turned up the collar of his mackinaw jacket and stared about him helplessly.

"It's a gloryus game yer runnin', Kid," cried Lon McFane. "All the percentage to the house an' niver a bit to the man that's buckin'. The Devil himself'd niver tackle such a cinch — and damned if I do."

There were chuckles, throttled in gurgling throats, and winks brushed away with the frost which rimed the eyelashes, as the men climbed the ice-notched bank and started across the street to the Post. But the long howl had drawn nearer, invested with a new note of menace. A woman screamed round the corner. There was a cry of, " Here he comes ! " Then an Indian boy, at the head of half a dozen frightened dogs, racing with death, dashed into the crowd. And behind came Yellow Fang, a bristle of hair and a flash of gray. Everybody but the Yankee fled. The Indian boy had tripped and fallen. Bettles stopped long enough to grip him by the slack of his furs, then headed for a pile of cordwood already occupied by a number of his comrades. Yellow Fang, doubling after one of the dogs, came leaping back. The fleeing animal, free of the rabies but crazed with fright, whipped Bettles off his feet and flashed on up the street. Malemute Kid took a flying shot at Yellow Fang. The mad dog whirled a half airspring, came down on his back, then, with a single leap, covered half the distance between himself and Bettles.

But the fatal spring was intercepted. Lon McFane leaped from the woodpile, countering him in midair. Over they rolled, Lon holding him by the throat at arm's length, blinking under the fetid slaver which sprayed his face.   Then Bettles, revolver in hand and coolly waiting a chance, settled the combat.

" 'T was a square game, Kid," Lon remarked, rising to his feet and shaking the snow from out his sleeves ; " with a fair percentage to meself that bucked it."

That night, while Lon McFane sought the forgiving arms of the Church in the direction of Father Roubeau's cabin, Malemute Kid and Scruff Mackenzie talked long to little purpose.

"But would you," persisted Mackenzie, " supposing they had fought ? "

" Have I ever broken my word ? "

" No ; but that is n't the point.   Answer the question.   Would you ? "

Malemute Kid straightened up.   " Scruff, I 've been asking myself that question ever since, and " —

" Well ? "

" Well, as yet, I have n't found the answer."

IN A FAR COUNTRY

WHEN a man journeys into a far country, he must be prepared to forget many of the things he has learned, and to acquire such customs as are inherent with existence in the new land; he must abandon the old ideals and the old gods, and oftentimes he must reverse the very codes by which his conduct has hitherto been shaped. To those who have the protean faculty of adaptability, the novelty of such change may even be a source of pleasure; but to those who happen to be hardened to the ruts in which they were created, the pressure of the altered environment is unbearable, and they chafe in body and in spirit under the new restrictions which they do not understand. This chafing is bound to act and react, producing divers evils and leading to various misfortunes. It were better for the man who cannot fit himself to the new groove to return to his own country; if he delay too long, he will surely die.

The man who turns his back upon the

comforts of an elder civilization, to face the savage youth, the primordial simplicity of the North, may estimate success at an inverse ratio to the quantity and quality of his hopelessly fixed habits. He will soon discover, if he be a fit candidate, that the material habits are the less important. The exchange of such things as a dainty menu for rough fare, of the stiff leather shoe for the soft, shapeless moccasin, of the feather bed for a couch in the snow, is after all a very easy matter. But his pinch will come in learning properly to shape his mind's attitude toward all things, and especially toward his fellow man. For the courtesies of ordinary life, he must substitute unselfishness, forbearance, and tolerance. Thus, and thus only, can he gain that pearl of great price, — true comradeship. He must not say "Thank you;" he must mean it without opening his mouth, and prove it by responding in kind. In short, he must substitute the deed for the word, the spirit for the letter.

When the world rang with the tale of Arctic gold, and the lure of the North gripped the heartstrings of men, Carter Weatherbee threw up his snug clerkship,

turned the half of his savings over to his
wife, and with the remainder bought an outfit.   There was no romance in his nature, —
the bondage of commerce had crushed all
that; he was simply tired of the ceaseless
grind, and wished to risk great hazards in
view of corresponding returns.   Like many
another fool, disdaining the old trails used
by the Northland pioneers for a score of
years, he hurried to Edmonton in the spring
of the year ; and there, unluckily for his
soul's welfare, he allied himself with a party
of men.

There was nothing unusual about this
party, except its plans.   Even its goal, like
that of all other parties, was the Klondike.
But the route it had mapped out to attain
that goal took away the breath of the hardi-
est native, born and bred to the vicissitudes
of the Northwest.   Even Jacques Baptiste,
born of a Chippewa woman and a renegade
voyageur (having raised his first whimpers
in a deerskin lodge north of the sixty-fifth
parallel, and had the same hushed by blissful
sucks of raw tallow), was surprised.   Though
he sold his services to them and agreed to
travel even to the never-opening ice, he shook

his head ominously whenever his advice was asked.

Percy Cuthfert's evil star must have been in the ascendant, for he, too, joined this company of argonauts. He was an ordinary man, with a bank account as deep as his culture, which is saying a good deal. He had no reason to embark on such a venture, — no reason in the world, save that he suffered from an abnormal development of sentimentality. He mistook this for the true spirit of romance and adventure. Many another man has done the like, and made as fatal a mistake.

The first break-up of spring found the party following the ice-run of Elk River. It was an imposing fleet, for the outfit was large, and they were accompanied by a disreputable contingent of half-breed *voyageurs* with their women and children. Day in and day out, they labored with the bateaux and canoes, fought mosquitoes and other kindred pests, or sweated and swore at the portages. Severe toil like this lays a man naked to the very roots of his soul, and ere Lake Athabasca was lost in the south, each member of the party had hoisted his true colors.

The two shirks and chronic grumblers were

Carter Weatherbee and Percy Cuthfert. The whole party complained less of its aches and pains than did either of them. Not once did they volunteer for the thousand and one petty duties of the camp. A bucket of water to be brought, an extra armful of wood to be chopped, the dishes to be washed and wiped, a search to be made through the outfit for some suddenly indispensable article, — and these two effete scions of civilization discovered sprains or blisters requiring instant attention. They were the first to turn in at night, with a score of tasks yet undone; the last to turn out in the morning, when the start should be in readiness before the breakfast was begun. They were the first to fall to at meal-time, the last to have a hand in the cooking; the first to dive for a slim delicacy, the last to discover they had added to their own another man's share. If they toiled at the oars, they slyly cut the water at each stroke and allowed the boat's momentum to float up the blade. They thought nobody noticed; but their comrades swore under their breaths and grew to hate them, while Jacques Baptiste sneered openly and damned them from morning till night. But Jacques Baptiste was no gentleman.

At the Great Slave, Hudson Bay dogs were purchased, and the fleet sank to the guards with its added burden of dried fish and pemmican. Then canoe and bateau answered to the swift current of the Mackenzie, and they plunged into the Great Barren Ground. Every likely-looking "feeder" was prospected, but the elusive "pay-dirt" danced ever to the north. At the Great Bear, overcome by the common dread of the Unknown Lands, their *voyageurs* began to desert, and Fort of Good Hope saw the last and bravest bending to the tow-lines as they bucked the current down which they had so treacherously glided. Jacques Baptiste alone remained. Had he not sworn to travel even to the never-opening ice?

The lying charts, compiled in main from hearsay, were now constantly consulted. And they felt the need of hurry, for the sun had already passed its northern solstice and was leading the winter south again. Skirting the shores of the bay, where the Mackenzie disembogues into the Arctic Ocean, they entered the mouth of the Little Peel River. Then began the arduous up-stream toil, and the two Incapables fared worse than ever. Tow-line and pole, paddle and tump-line, rapids and portages, — such tortures served to give the one a deep disgust for great hazards, and printed for the other a fiery text on the true romance of adventure. One day they waxed mutinous, and being vilely cursed by Jacques Baptiste, turned, as worms sometimes will. But the half-breed thrashed the twain, and sent them, bruised and bleeding, about their work. It was the first time either had been man-handled.

Abandoning their river craft at the headwaters of the Little Peel, they consumed the rest of the summer in the great portage over the Mackenzie watershed to the West Rat. This little stream fed the Porcupine, which in turn joined the Yukon where that mighty highway of the North countermarches on the Arctic Circle. But they had lost in the race with winter, and one day they tied their rafts to the thick eddy-ice and hurried their goods ashore. That night the river jammed and broke several times; the following morning it had fallen asleep for good.

" We can't be more 'n four hundred miles from the Yukon," concluded Sloper, multiplying his thumb nails by the scale of the map. The council, in which the two Incapables had whined to excellent disadvantage, was drawing to a close.

"Hudson Bay Post, long time ago. No use um now."   Jacques Baptiste's father had made the trip for the Fur Company in the old days, incidentally marking the trail with a couple of frozen toes.

"Sufferin' cracky!" cried another of the party.   "No whites?"

"Nary white," Sloper sententiously affirmed; "but it's only five hundred more up the Yukon to Dawson. Call it a rough thousand from here."

Weatherbee and Cuthfert groaned in chorus.

"How long 'll that take, Baptiste?"

The half-breed figured for a moment. "Workum like hell, no man play out, ten — twenty — forty — fifty days. Um babies come" (designating the Incapables), "no can tell. Mebbe when hell freeze over; mebbe not then."

The manufacture of snowshoes and moccasins ceased. Somebody called the name of an absent member, who came out of an ancient cabin at the edge of the camp-fire and joined them. The cabin was one of the many mysteries which lurk in the vast recesses of the North. Built when and by whom, no man could tell. Two graves in the open, piled high with stones, perhaps contained the secret of those early wanderers. But whose hand had piled the stones?

The moment had come. Jacques Baptiste paused in the fitting of a harness and pinned the struggling dog in the snow. The cook made mute protest for delay, threw a handful of bacon into a noisy pot of beans, then came to attention. Sloper rose to his feet. His body was a ludicrous contrast to the healthy physiques of the Incapables. Yellow and weak, fleeing from a South American fever-hole, he had not broken his flight across the zones, and was still able to toil with men. His weight was probably ninety pounds, with the heavy hunting-knife thrown in, and his grizzled hair told of a prime which had ceased to be. The fresh young muscles of either Weatherbee or Cuthfert were equal to ten times the endeavor of his; yet he could walk them into the earth in a day's journey. And all this day he had whipped his stronger comrades into venturing a thousand miles of the

stiffest hardship man can conceive. He was
the incarnation of the unrest of his race, and
the old Teutonic stubbornness, dashed with
the quick grasp and action of the Yankee,
held the flesh in the bondage of the spirit.

"All those in favor of going on with the
dogs as soon as the ice sets, say ay."

"Ay!" rang out eight voices, — voices destined to string a trail of oaths along many a
hundred miles of pain.

"Contrary minded?"

"No!" For the first time the Incapables
were united without some compromise of personal interests.

"And what are you going to do about it?"
Weatherbee added belligerently.

"Majority rule! Majority rule!" clamored
the rest of the party.

"I know the expedition is liable to fall
through if you don't come," Sloper replied
sweetly; "but I guess, if we try real hard,
we can manage to do without you. What do
you say, boys?"

The sentiment was cheered to the echo.

"But I say, you know," Cuthfert ventured
apprehensively; "what's a chap like me to
do?"

" Ain't you coming with us ? "

" No-o."

" Then do as you damn well please. We won't have nothing to say."

" Kind o' calkilate yuh might settle it with that canoodlin' pardner of yourn," suggested a heavy-going Westerner from the Dakotas, at the same time pointing out Weatherbee. " He 'll be shore to ask yuh what yur a-goin' to do when it comes to cookin' an' gatherin' the wood."

" Then we 'll consider it all arranged," concluded Sloper. " We 'll pull out to-morrow, if we camp within five miles, — just to get everything in running order and remember if we 've forgotten anything."

The sleds groaned by on their steel-shod runners, and the dogs strained low in the harnesses in which they were born to die. Jacques Baptiste paused by the side of Sloper to get a last glimpse of the cabin. The smoke curled up pathetically from the Yukon stovepipe. The two Incapables were watching them from the doorway.

Sloper laid his hand on the other's shoulder.

"Jacques Baptiste, did you ever hear of the Kilkenny cats?"

The half-breed shook his head.

"Well, my friend and good comrade, the Kilkenny cats fought till neither hide, nor hair, nor yowl, was left. You understand? —till nothing was left. Very good. Now, these two men don't like work. They won't work. We know that. They'll be all alone in that cabin all winter,—a mighty long, dark winter. Kilkenny cats,—well?"

The Frenchman in Baptiste shrugged his shoulders, but the Indian in him was silent. Nevertheless, it was an eloquent shrug, pregnant with prophecy.

Things prospered in the little cabin at first. The rough badinage of their comrades had made Weatherbee and Cuthfert conscious of the mutual responsibility which had devolved upon them; besides, there was not so much work after all for two healthy men. And the removal of the cruel whip-hand, or in other words the bulldozing half-breed, had brought with it a joyous reaction. At first, each strove to outdo the other, and they performed petty tasks with an unction which would have opened the eyes of their comrades who were now wearing out bodies and souls on the Long Trail.

All care was banished. The forest, which shouldered in upon them from three sides, was an inexhaustible woodyard. A few yards from their door slept the Porcupine, and a hole through its winter robe formed a bubbling spring of water, crystal clear and painfully cold. But they soon grew to find fault with even that. The hole would persist in freezing up, and thus gave them many a miserable hour of ice-chopping. The unknown builders of the cabin had extended the side-logs so as to support a cache at the rear. In this was stored the bulk of the party's provisions. Food there was, without stint, for three times the men who were fated to live upon it. But the most of it was of the kind which built up brawn and sinew, but did not tickle the palate. True, there was sugar in plenty for two ordinary men; but these two were little else than children. They early discovered the virtues of hot water judiciously saturated with sugar, and they prodigally swam their flapjacks and soaked their crusts in the rich, white syrup. Then coffee and tea, and especially the dried fruits, made disastrous inroads upon it. The first words they had were over the sugar question. And it is a really serious thing when two men, wholly dependent upon each other for company, begin to quarrel.

Weatherbee loved to discourse blatantly on politics, while Cuthfert, who had been prone to clip his coupons and let the commonwealth jog on as best it might, either ignored the subject or delivered himself of startling epigrams. But the clerk was too obtuse to appreciate the clever shaping of thought, and this waste of ammunition irritated Cuthfert. He had been used to blinding people by his brilliancy, and it worked him quite a hardship, this loss of an audience. He felt personally aggrieved and unconsciously held his mutton-head companion responsible for it.

Save existence, they had nothing in common, — came in touch on no single point. Weatherbee was a clerk who had known naught but clerking all his life; Cuthfert was a master of arts, a dabbler in oils, and had written not a little. The one was a lower-class man who considered himself a

gentleman, and the other was a gentleman
who knew himself to be such. From this it
may be remarked that a man can be a gentleman without possessing the first instinct of
true comradeship. The clerk was as sensu-
ous as the other was æsthetic, and his love
adventures, told at great length and chiefly
coined from his imagination, affected the
supersensitive master of arts in the same way
as so many whiffs of sewer gas. He deemed
the clerk a filthy, uncultured brute, whose
place was in the muck with the swine, and
told him so; and he was reciprocally informed
that he was a milk-and-water sissy and a cad.
Weatherbee could not have defined "cad"
for his life; but it satisfied its purpose, which
after all seems the main point in life.

Weatherbee flatted every third note and
sang such songs as "The Boston Burglar"
and "The Handsome Cabin Boy," for hours
at a time, while Cuthfert wept with rage, till
he could stand it no longer and fled into the
outer cold. But there was no escape. The
intense frost could not be endured for long
at a time, and the little cabin crowded them
— beds, stove, table, and all — into a space
of ten by twelve. The very presence of

either became a personal affront to the other, and they lapsed into sullen silences which increased in length and strength as the days went by. Occasionally, the flash of an eye or the curl of a lip got the better of them, though they strove to wholly ignore each other during these mute periods. And a great wonder sprang up in the breast of each, as to how God had ever come to create the other.

With little to do, time became an intolerable burden to them. This naturally made them still lazier. They sank into a physical lethargy which there was no escaping, and which made them rebel at the performance of the smallest chore. One morning when it was his turn to cook the common breakfast, Weatherbee rolled out of his blankets, and to the snoring of his companion, lighted first the slush-lamp and then the fire. The kettles were frozen hard, and there was no water in the cabin with which to wash. But he did not mind that. Waiting for it to thaw, he sliced the bacon and plunged into the hateful task of bread-making. Cuthfert had been slyly watching through his half-closed lids. Consequently there was a scene, in which

they fervently blessed each other, and agreed,
thenceforth, that each do his own cooking. A
week later, Cuthfert neglected his morning
ablutions, but none the less complacently ate
the meal which he had cooked. Weatherbee
grinned. After that the foolish custom of
washing passed out of their lives.

As the sugar-pile and other little luxuries
dwindled, they began to be afraid they were
not getting their proper shares, and in order
that they might not be robbed, they fell to
gorging themselves. The luxuries suffered
in this gluttonous contest, as did also the
men. In the absence of fresh vegetables
and exercise, their blood became impover-
ished, and a loathsome, purplish rash crept
over their bodies. Yet they refused to heed
the warning. Next, their muscles and joints
began to swell, the flesh turning black, while
their mouths, gums, and lips took on the
color of rich cream. Instead of being drawn
together by their misery, each gloated over
the other's symptoms as the scurvy took its
course.

They lost all regard for personal appearance, and for that matter, common decency.
The cabin became a pigpen, and never once

were the beds made or fresh pine boughs laid underneath. Yet they could not keep to their blankets, as they would have wished; for the frost was inexorable, and the fire box consumed much fuel. The hair of their heads and faces grew long and shaggy, while their garments would have disgusted a ragpicker. But they did not care. They were sick, and there was no one to see; besides, it was very painful to move about.

To all this was added a new trouble, — the Fear of the North. This Fear was the joint child of the Great Cold and the Great Silence, and was born in the darkness of December, when the sun dipped below the southern horizon for good. It affected them according to their natures. Weatherbee fell prey to the grosser superstitions, and did his best to resurrect the spirits which slept in the forgotten graves. It was a fascinating thing, and in his dreams they came to him from out of the cold, and snuggled into his blankets, and told him of their toils and troubles ere they died. He shrank away from the clammy contact as they drew closer and twined their frozen limbs about him, and when they whispered in his ear of things to come, the cabin rang with his frightened shrieks. Cuthfert did not understand, — for they no longer spoke, — and when thus awakened he invariably grabbed for his revolver. Then he would sit up in bed, shivering nervously, with the weapon trained on the unconscious dreamer. Cuthfert deemed the man going mad, and so came to fear for his life.

His own malady assumed a less concrete form. The mysterious artisan who had laid the cabin, log by log, had pegged a windvane to the ridge-pole. Cuthfert noticed it always pointed south, and one day, irritated by its steadfastness of purpose, he turned it toward the east. He watched eagerly, but never a breath came by to disturb it. Then he turned the vane to the north, swearing never again to touch it till the wind did blow. But the air frightened him with its unearthly calm, and he often rose in the middle of the night to see if the vane had veered, — ten degrees would have satisfied him. But no, it poised above him as unchangeable as fate. His imagination ran riot, till it became to him a fetich. Sometimes he followed the path it pointed across the dismal dominions, and allowed his soul to become saturated with the Fear. He dwelt upon the unseen and the unknown till the burden of eternity appeared to be crushing him. Everything in the Northland had that crushing effect, — the absence of life and motion; the darkness; the infinite peace of the brooding land; the ghastly silence, which made the echo of each heart-beat a sacrilege; the solemn forest which seemed to guard an awful, inexpressible something, which neither word nor thought could compass.

The world he had so recently left, with its busy nations and great enterprises, seemed very far away. Recollections occasionally obtruded, — recollections of marts and galleries and crowded thoroughfares, of evening dress and social functions, of good men and dear women he had known, — but they were dim memories of a life he had lived long centuries agone, on some other planet. This phantasm was the Reality. Standing beneath the wind-vane, his eyes fixed on the polar skies, he could not bring himself to realize that the Southland really existed, that at that very moment it was a-roar with life and action. There was no Southland, no men being born of women, no giving and taking in marriage. Beyond his bleak sky-line there stretched vast solitudes, and beyond these still vaster solitudes. There were no lands of sunshine, heavy with the perfume of flowers. Such things were only old dreams of paradise. The sunlands of the West and the spicelands of the East, the smiling Arcadias and blissful Islands of the Blest, — ha! ha! His laughter split the void and shocked him with its unwonted sound. There was no sun. This was the Universe, dead and cold and dark, and he its only citizen. Weatherbee? At such moments Weatherbee did not count. He was a Caliban, a monstrous phantom, fettered to him for untold ages, the penalty of some forgotten crime.

He lived with Death among the dead, emasculated by the sense of his own insignificance, crushed by the passive mastery of the slumbering ages. The magnitude of all things appalled him. Everything partook of the superlative save himself, — the perfect cessation of wind and motion, the immensity of the snow-covered wilderness, the height of the sky and the depth of the silence. That wind-vane, — if it would only move. If a thunderbolt would fall, or the forest flare up in flame. The rolling up of the heavens as a scroll, the crash of Doom — anything, anything! But no, nothing moved; the Silence crowded in, and the Fear of the North laid icy fingers on his heart.

Once, like another Crusoe, by the edge of the river he came upon a track, — the faint tracery of a snowshoe rabbit on the delicate snow-crust. It was a revelation. There was life in the Northland. He would follow it, look upon it, gloat over it. He forgot his swollen muscles, plunging through the deep snow in an ecstasy of anticipation. The forest swallowed him up, and the brief midday twilight vanished; but he pursued his quest till exhausted nature asserted itself and laid him helpless in the snow. There he groaned and cursed his folly, and knew the track to be the fancy of his brain; and late that night he dragged himself into the cabin on hands and knees, his cheeks frozen and a strange numbness about his feet. Weatherbee grinned malevolently, but made no offer to help him. He thrust needles into his toes and thawed them out by the stove. A week later mortification set in.

But the clerk had his own troubles. The

dead men came out of their graves more frequently now, and rarely left him, waking or sleeping. He grew to wait and dread their coming, never passing the twin cairns without a shudder. One night they came to him in his sleep and led him forth to an appointed task. Frightened into inarticulate horror, he awoke between the heaps of stones and fled wildly to the cabin. But he had lain there for some time, for his feet and cheeks were also frozen.

Sometimes he became frantic at their insistent presence, and danced about the cabin, cutting the empty air with an axe, and smashing everything within reach. During these ghostly encounters, Cuthfert huddled into his blankets and followed the madman about with a cocked revolver, ready to shoot him if he came too near. But, recovering from one of these spells, the clerk noticed the weapon trained upon him. His suspicions were aroused, and thenceforth he, too, lived in fear of his life. They watched each other closely after that, and faced about in startled fright whenever either passed behind the other's back. This apprehensiveness became a mania which controlled them even in their sleep. Through mutual fear they tacitly let the slush-lamp burn all night, and saw to a plentiful supply of bacon-grease before retiring. The slightest movement on the part of one was sufficient to arouse the other, and many a still watch their gazes countered as they shook beneath their blankets with fingers on the trigger-guards.

What with the Fear of the North, the mental strain, and the ravages of the disease, they lost all semblance of humanity, taking on the appearance of wild beasts, hunted and desperate. Their cheeks and noses, as an aftermath of the freezing, had turned black. Their frozen toes had begun to drop away at the first and second joints. Every movement brought pain, but the fire box was insatiable, wringing a ransom of torture from their miserable bodies. Day in, day out, it demanded its food, — a veritable pound of flesh, — and they dragged themselves into the forest to chop wood on their knees. Once, crawling thus in search of dry sticks, unknown to each other they entered a thicket from opposite sides. Suddenly, without warning, two peering death's-heads confronted each other. Suffering had so transformed

them that recognition was impossible. They
sprang to their feet, shrieking with terror,
and dashed away on their mangled stumps;
and falling at the cabin door, they clawed
and scratched like demons till they discovered
their mistake.

Occasionally they lapsed normal, and during one of these sane intervals, the chief
bone of contention, the sugar, had been
divided equally between them. They guarded
their separate sacks, stored up in the cache,
with jealous eyes; for there were but a few
cupfuls left, and they were totally devoid of
faith in each other. But one day Cuthfert
made a mistake. Hardly able to move, sick
with pain, with his head swimming and eyes
blinded, he crept into the cache, sugar canis-
ter in hand, and mistook Weatherbee's sack
for his own.

January had been born but a few days
when this occurred. The sun had some time
since passed its lowest southern declination,
and at meridian now threw flaunting streaks
of yellow light upon the northern sky. On
the day following his mistake with the sugar-
bag, Cuthfert found himself feeling better,

both in body and in spirit. As noontime drew near and the day brightened, he dragged himself outside to feast on the evanescent glow, which was to him an earnest of the sun's future intentions. Weatherbee was also feeling somewhat better, and crawled out beside him. They propped themselves in the snow beneath the moveless wind-vane, and waited.

The stillness of death was about them. In other climes, when nature falls into such moods, there is a subdued air of expectancy, a waiting for some small voice to take up the broken strain. Not so in the North. The two men had lived seeming æons in this ghostly peace. They could remember no song of the past; they could conjure no song of the future. This unearthly calm had always been, — the tranquil silence of eternity.

Their eyes were fixed upon the north. Unseen, behind their backs, behind the towering mountains to the south, the sun swept toward the zenith of another sky than theirs. Sole spectators of the mighty canvas, they watched the false dawn slowly grow. A faint flame began to glow and smoulder. It deepened in intensity, ringing the changes of reddish-yel-

low, purple, and saffron. So bright did it
become that Cuthfert thought the sun must
surely be behind it, — a miracle, the sun rising in the north! Suddenly, without warning and without fading, the canvas was swept
clean. There was no color in the sky. The
light had gone out of the day. They caught
their breaths in half-sobs. But lo! the air
was a-glint with particles of scintillating
frost, and there, to the north, the wind-vane
lay in vague outline on the snow. A shadow!
A shadow! It was exactly midday. They
jerked their heads hurriedly to the south.
A golden rim peeped over the mountain's
snowy shoulder, smiled upon them an instant,
then dipped from sight again.

There were tears in their eyes as they
sought each other. A strange softening came
over them. They felt irresistibly drawn
toward each other. The sun was coming
back again. It would be with them to-morrow, and the next day, and the next. And
it would stay longer every visit, and a time
would come when it would ride their heaven
day and night, never once dropping below
the sky-line. There would be no night.
The ice-locked winter would be broken; the

winds would blow and the forests answer;
the land would bathe in the blessed sunshine,
and life renew. Hand in hand, they would
quit this horrid dream and journey back to
the Southland. They lurched blindly forward, and their hands met, — their poor
maimed hands, swollen and distorted beneath
their mittens.

But the promise was destined to remain
unfulfilled. The Northland is the Northland, and men work out their souls by strange
rules, which other men, who have not journeyed into far countries, cannot come to
understand.

An hour later, Cuthfert put a pan of bread
into the oven, and fell to speculating on what
the surgeons could do with his feet when he
got back. Home did not seem so very far
away now. Weatherbee was rummaging in
the cache. Of a sudden, he raised a whirlwind of blasphemy, which in turn ceased with
startling abruptness. The other man had
robbed his sugar-sack. Still, things might
have happened differently, had not the two
dead men come out from under the stones
and hushed the hot words in his throat.

They led him quite gently from the cache, which he forgot to close. That consummation was reached ; that something they had whispered to him in his dreams was about to happen. They guided him gently, very gently, to the woodpile, where they put the axe in his hands. Then they helped him shove open the cabin door, and he felt sure they shut it after him, — at least he heard it slam and the latch fall sharply into place. And he knew they were waiting just without, waiting for him to do his task.

"Carter! I say, Carter!"

Percy Cuthfert was frightened at the look on the clerk's face, and he made haste to put the table between them.

Carter Weatherbee followed, without haste and without enthusiasm. There was neither pity nor passion in his face, but rather the patient, stolid look of one who has certain work to do and goes about it methodically.

"I say, what's the matter?"

The clerk dodged back, cutting off his retreat to the door, but never opening his mouth.

"I say, Carter, I say; let's talk. There's a good chap."

The master of arts was thinking rapidly, now, shaping a skillful flank movement on the bed where his Smith & Wesson lay. Keeping his eyes on the madman, he rolled backward on the bunk, at the same time clutching the pistol.

"Carter!"

The powder flashed full in Weatherbee's face, but he swung his weapon and leaped forward. The axe bit deeply at the base of the spine, and Percy Cuthfert felt all consciousness of his lower limbs leave him. Then the clerk fell heavily upon him, clutching him by the throat with feeble fingers. The sharp bite of the axe had caused Cuthfert to drop the pistol, and as his lungs panted for release, he fumbled aimlessly for it among the blankets. Then he remembered. He slid a hand up the clerk's belt to the sheath-knife; and they drew very close to each other in that last clinch.

Percy Cuthfert felt his strength leave him. The lower portion of his body was useless. The inert weight of Weatherbee crushed him, — crushed him and pinned him there like a bear under a trap. The cabin became filled with a familiar odor, and he knew the bread to be burning. Yet what did it matter? He would never need it. And there were all of six cupfuls of sugar in the cache, — if he had foreseen this he would not have been so saving the last several days. Would the wind-vane ever move? It might even be veering now. Why not? Had he not seen the sun to-day? He would go and see. No; it was impossible to move. He had not thought the clerk so heavy a man.

How quickly the cabin cooled! The fire must be out. The cold was forcing in. It must be below zero already, and the ice creeping up the inside of the door. He could not see it, but his past experience enabled him to gauge its progress by the cabin's temperature. The lower hinge must be white ere now. Would the tale of this ever reach the world? How would his friends take it? They would read it over their coffee, most likely, and talk it over at the clubs. He could see them very clearly. "Poor Old Cuthfert," they murmured; "not such a bad sort of a chap, after all." He smiled at their eulogies, and passed on in search of a Turkish bath. It was the same old crowd upon the streets. Strange, they did not notice his moosehide moccasins and tattered German socks! He would take a cab. And after the bath a shave would not be bad. No; he would eat first. Steak, and potatoes, and green things, — how fresh it all was! And what was that? Squares of honey, streaming liquid amber! But why did they bring so much? Ha! ha! he could never eat it all. Shine! Why certainly. He put his foot on the box. The bootblack looked curiously up at him, and he remembered his moosehide moccasins and went away hastily.

Hark! The wind-vane must be surely spinning. No; a mere singing in his ears. That was all, — a mere singing. The ice must have passed the latch by now. More likely the upper hinge was covered. Between the moss-chinked roof-poles, little points of frost began to appear. How slowly they grew! No; not so slowly. There was a new one, and there another. Two — three — four; they were coming too fast to count. There were two growing together. And there, a third had joined them. Why, there were no more spots. They had run together and formed a sheet.

Well, he would have company. If Gabriel

ever broke the silence of the North, they
would stand together, hand in hand, before
the great White Throne.   And God would
judge them, God would judge them!

Then Percy Cuthfert closed his eyes and
dropped off to sleep.

TO THE MAN ON TRAIL

"Dump it in."

"But I say, Kid, is n't that going it a little too strong? Whiskey and alcohol's bad enough; but when it comes to brandy and pepper-sauce and " —

"Dump it in. Who's making this punch, anyway?" And Malemute Kid smiled benignantly through the clouds of steam. "By the time you've been in this country as long as I have, my son, and lived on rabbit-tracks and salmon-belly, you'll learn that Christmas comes only once per annum. And a Christmas without punch is sinking a hole to bedrock with nary a pay-streak."

"Stack up on that fer a high cyard," approved Big Jim Belden, who had come down from his claim on Mazy May to spend Christmas, and who, as every one knew, had been living the two months past on straight moose-meat. "Hain't fergot the *hooch* we-uns made on the Tanana, hev yeh?"

"Well, I guess yes. Boys, it would have

done your hearts good to see that whole tribe fighting drunk — and all because of a glorious ferment of sugar and sour dough. That was before your time," Malemute Kid said as he turned to Stanley Prince, a young mining expert who had been in two years. "No white women in the country then, and Mason wanted to get married. Ruth's father was chief of the Tananas, and objected, like the rest of the tribe. Stiff? Why, I used my last pound of sugar; finest work in that line I ever did in my life. You should have seen the chase, down the river and across the portage."

"But the squaw?" asked Louis Savoy, the tall French-Canadian, becoming interested; for he had heard of this wild deed, when at Forty Mile the preceding winter.

Then Malemute Kid, who was a born raconteur, told the unvarnished tale of the Northland Lochinvar. More than one rough adventurer of the North felt his heartstrings draw closer, and experienced vague yearnings for the sunnier pastures of the Southland, where life promised something more than a barren struggle with cold and death.

"We struck the Yukon just behind the

first ice-run," he concluded, " and the tribe only a quarter of an hour behind. But that saved us ; for the second run broke the jam above and shut them out. When they finally got into Nuklukyeto, the whole Post was ready for them. And as to the foregathering, ask Father Roubeau here : he performed the ceremony."

The Jesuit took the pipe from his lips, but could only express his gratification with patriarchal smiles, while Protestant and Catholic vigorously applauded.

" By gar ! " ejaculated Louis Savoy, who seemed overcome by the romance of it. " La petite squaw ; mon Mason brav. By gar ! "

Then, as the first tin cups of punch went round, Bettles the Unquenchable sprang to his feet and struck up his favorite drinking song : —

> " There 's Henry Ward Beecher
>   And Sunday-school teachers,
>   All drink of the sassafras root ;
>   But you bet all the same,
>   If it had its right name,
>   It 's the juice of the forbidden fruit."

" Oh the juice of the forbidden fruit,"

roared out the Bacchanalian chorus, —

"Oh the juice of the forbidden fruit ;
   But you bet all the same,
   If it had its right name,
It 's the juice of the forbidden fruit."

Malemute Kid's frightful concoction did its work ; the men of the camps and trails unbent in its genial glow, and jest and song and tales of past adventure went round the board. Aliens from a dozen lands, they toasted each and all. It was the Englishman, Prince, who pledged " Uncle Sam, the precocious infant of the New World ; " the Yankee, Bettles, who drank to " The Queen, God bless her ; " and together, Savoy and Meyers, the German trader, clanged their cups to Alsace and Lorraine.

Then Malemute Kid arose, cup in hand, and glanced at the greased-paper window, where the frost stood full three inches thick. " A health to the man on trail this night ; may his grub hold out ; may his dogs keep their legs ; may his matches never miss fire."

Crack ! Crack ! — they heard the familiar music of the dogwhip, the whining howl of the Malemutes, and the crunch of a sled as it drew up to the cabin. Conversation languished while they waited the issue.

"An old-timer; cares for his dogs and then himself," whispered Malemute Kid to Prince, as they listened to the snapping jaws and the wolfish snarls and yelps of pain which proclaimed to their practiced ears that the stranger was beating back their dogs while he fed his own.

Then came the expected knock, sharp and confident, and the stranger entered. Dazzled by the light, he hesitated a moment at the door, giving to all a chance for scrutiny. He was a striking personage, and a most picturesque one, in his Arctic dress of wool and fur. Standing six foot two or three, with proportionate breadth of shoulders and depth of chest, his smooth-shaven face nipped by the cold to a gleaming pink, his long lashes and eyebrows white with ice, and the ear and neck flaps of his great wolfskin cap loosely raised, he seemed, of a verity, the Frost King, just stepped in out of the night. Clasped outside his mackinaw jacket, a beaded belt held two large Colt's revolvers and a hunting-knife, while he carried, in addition to the inevitable dogwhip, a smokeless rifle of the largest bore and latest pattern. As he came forward, for all his step was firm and elastic, they could see that fatigue bore heavily upon him.

An awkward silence had fallen, but his hearty " What cheer, my lads ? " put them quickly at ease, and the next instant Malemute Kid and he had gripped hands. Though they had never met, each had heard of the other, and the recognition was mutual. A sweeping introduction and a mug of punch were forced upon him before he could explain his errand.

" How long since that basket-sled, with three men and eight dogs, passed ? " he asked.

" An even two days ahead. Are you after them ? "

" Yes ; my team. Run them off under my very nose, the cusses. I 've gained two days on them already, — pick them up on the next run."

" Reckon they 'll show spunk ? " asked Belden, in order to keep up the conversation, for Malemute Kid already had the coffee-pot on and was busily frying bacon and moose-meat.

The stranger significantly tapped his revolvers.

"When 'd yeh leave Dawson?"

"Twelve o'clock."

"Last night?" — as a matter of course.

"To-day."

A murmur of surprise passed round the circle. And well it might; for it was just midnight, and seventy-five miles of rough river trail was not to be sneered at for a twelve hours' run.

The talk soon became impersonal, however, harking back to the trails of childhood. As the young stranger ate of the rude fare, Malemute Kid attentively studied his face. Nor was he long in deciding that it was fair, honest, and open, and that he liked it. Still youthful, the lines had been firmly traced by toil and hardship. Though genial in conversation, and mild when at rest, the blue eyes gave promise of the hard steel-glitter which comes when called into action, especially against odds. The heavy jaw and square-cut chin demonstrated rugged pertinacity and indomitability. Nor, though the attributes of the lion were there, was there wanting the certain softness, the hint of womanliness, which bespoke the emotional nature.

"So thet 's how me an' the ol' woman got

spliced," said Belden, concluding the exciting tale of his courtship. "'Here we be, dad,' sez she. 'An' may yeh be damned,' sez he to her, an' then to me, 'Jim, yeh — yeh git outen them good duds o' yourn; I want a right peart slice o' thet forty acre ploughed 'fore dinner.' An' then he turns on her an' sez, ' An' yeh, Sal; yeh sail inter them dishes.' An' then he sort o' sniffled an' kissed her. An' I was thet happy, — but he seen me an' roars out, ' Yeh, Jim!' An' yeh bet I dusted fer the barn."

"Any kids waiting for you back in the States?" asked the stranger.

"Nope; Sal died 'fore any come. Thet's why I'm here." Belden abstractedly began to light his pipe, which had failed to go out, and then brightened up with, "How 'bout yerself, stranger, — married man?"

For reply, he opened his watch, slipped it from the thong which served for a chain, and passed it over. Belden pricked up the slush-lamp, surveyed the inside of the case critically, and swearing admiringly to himself, handed it over to Louis Savoy. With numerous "By gars!" he finally surrendered it to Prince, and they noticed that his hands trembled and his eyes took on a peculiar softness. And so it passed from horny hand to horny hand — the pasted photograph of a woman, the clinging kind that such men fancy, with a babe at the breast. Those who had not yet seen the wonder were keen with curiosity; those who had, became silent and retrospective. They could face the pinch of famine, the grip of scurvy, or the quick death by field or flood; but the pictured semblance of a stranger woman and child made women and children of them all.

"Never have seen the youngster yet, — he's a boy, she says, and two years old," said the stranger as he received the treasure back. A lingering moment he gazed upon it, then snapped the case and turned away, but not quick enough to hide the restrained rush of tears.

Malemute Kid led him to a bunk and bade him turn in.

"Call me at four, sharp. Don't fail me," were his last words, and a moment later he was breathing in the heaviness of exhausted sleep.

"By Jove! he's a plucky chap," commented Prince. "Three hours' sleep after seventy-five miles with the dogs, and then the trail again. Who is he, Kid?"

"Jack Westondale. Been in going on three years, with nothing but the name of working like a horse, and any amount of bad luck to his credit. I never knew him, but Sitka Charley told me about him."

"It seems hard that a man with a sweet young wife like his should be putting in his years in this God-forsaken hole, where every year counts two on the outside."

"The trouble with him is clean grit and stubbornness. He's cleaned up twice with a stake, but lost it both times."

Here the conversation was broken off by an uproar from Bettles, for the effect had begun to wear away. And soon the bleak years of monotonous grub and deadening toil were being forgotten in rough merriment. Malemute Kid alone seemed unable to lose himself, and cast many an anxious look at his watch. Once he put on his mittens and beaver-skin cap, and leaving the cabin, fell to rummaging about in the cache.

Nor could he wait the hour designated; for he was fifteen minutes ahead of time in rousing his guest. The young giant had stiffened badly, and brisk rubbing was necessary to bring him to his feet. He tottered painfully out of the cabin, to find his dogs harnessed and everything ready for the start. The company wished him good luck and a short chase, while Father Roubeau, hurriedly blessing him, led the stampede for the cabin; and small wonder, for it is not good to face seventy-four degrees below zero with naked ears and hands.

Malemute Kid saw him to the main trail, and there, gripping his hand heartily, gave him advice.

" You 'll find a hundred pounds of salmon-eggs on the sled," he said. " The dogs will go as far on that as with one hundred and fifty of fish, and you can't get dog-food at Pelly, as you probably expected." The stranger started, and his eyes flashed, but he did not interrupt. " You can't get an ounce of food for dog or man till you reach Five Fingers, and that 's a stiff two hundred miles. Watch out for open water on the Thirty Mile River, and be sure you take the big cut-off above Le Barge."

" How did you know it ? Surely the news can't be ahead of me already ? "

"I don't know it; and what's more, I don't want to know it. But you never owned that team you're chasing. Sitka Charley sold it to them last spring. But he sized you up to me as square once, and I believe him. I've seen your face; I like it. And I've seen — why, damn you, hit the high places for salt water and that wife of yours, and" — Here the Kid unmittened and jerked out his sack.

"No; I don't need it," and the tears froze on his cheeks as he convulsively gripped Malemute Kid's hand.

"Then don't spare the dogs; cut them out of the traces as fast as they drop; buy them, and think they're cheap at ten dollars a pound. You can get them at Five Fingers, Little Salmon, and the Hootalinqua. And watch out for wet feet," was his parting advice. "Keep a-traveling up to twenty-five, but if it gets below that, build a fire and change your socks."

Fifteen minutes had barely elapsed when the jingle of bells announced new arrivals. The door opened, and a mounted policeman of the Northwest Territory entered, followed

by two half-breed dog-drivers. Like Westondale, they were heavily armed and showed
signs of fatigue. The half-breeds had been
born to the trail, and bore it easily; but the
young policeman was badly exhausted. Still,
the dogged obstinacy of his race held him to
the pace he had set, and would hold him till
he dropped in his tracks.

"When did Westondale pull out?" he
asked. "He stopped here, did n't he?"
This was supererogatory, for the tracks told
their own tale too well.

Malemute Kid had caught Belden's eye,
and he, scenting the wind, replied evasively,
"A right peart while back."

"Come, my man; speak up," the policeman admonished.

"Yeh seem to want him right smart. Hez
he ben gittin' cantankerous down Dawson
way?"

"Held up Harry McFarland's for forty
thousand; exchanged it at the P. C. store
for a check on Seattle; and who 's to stop the
cashing of it if we don't overtake him?
When did he pull out?"

Every eye suppressed its excitement, for
Malemute Kid had given the cue, and the

young officer encountered wooden faces on every hand.

Striding over to Prince, he put the question to him. Though it hurt him, gazing into the frank, earnest face of his fellow countryman, he replied inconsequentially on the state of the trail.

Then he espied Father Roubeau, who could not lie. " A quarter of an hour ago," the priest answered ; " but he had four hours' rest for himself and dogs."

" Fifteen minutes' start, and he 's fresh ! My God ! " The poor fellow staggered back, half fainting from exhaustion and disappointment, murmuring something about the run from Dawson in ten hours and the dogs being played out.

Malemute Kid forced a mug of punch upon him ; then he turned for the door, ordering the dog-drivers to follow. But the warmth and promise of rest were too tempting, and they objected strenuously. The Kid was conversant with their French patois, and followed it anxiously.

They swore that the dogs were gone up ; that Siwash and Babette would have to be shot before the first mile was covered ; that the rest were almost as bad; and that it would be better for all hands to rest up.

" Lend me five dogs?" he asked, turning to Malemute Kid.

But the Kid shook his head.

" I'll sign a check on Captain Constantine for five thousand, — here's my papers, — I'm authorized to draw at my own discretion."

Again the silent refusal.

" Then I'll requisition them in the name of the Queen."

Smiling incredulously, the Kid glanced at his well-stocked arsenal, and the Englishman, realizing his impotency, turned for the door. But the dog-drivers still objecting, he whirled upon them fiercely, calling them women and curs. The swart face of the older half-breed flushed angrily, as he drew himself up and promised in good, round terms that he would travel his leader off his legs, and would then be delighted to plant him in the snow.

The young officer — and it required his whole will — walked steadily to the door, exhibiting a freshness he did not possess. But they all knew and appreciated his proud effort ; nor could he veil the twinges of agony that shot across his face. Covered with

frost, the dogs were curled up in the snow,
and it was almost impossible to get them to
their feet. The poor brutes whined under
the stinging lash, for the dog-drivers were
angry and cruel ; nor till Babette, the leader,
was cut from the traces, could they break out
the sled and get under way.

"A dirty scoundrel and a liar!" "By
gar! him no good!" "A thief!" "Worse
than an Indian!" It was evident that they
were angry — first, at the way they had been
deceived ; and second, at the outraged ethics
of the Northland, where honesty, above all,
was man's prime jewel. "An' we gave the
cuss a hand, after knowin' what he'd did."
All eyes were turned accusingly upon Malemute Kid, who rose from the corner where
he had been making Babette comfortable,
and silently emptied the bowl for a final
round of punch.

"It's a cold night, boys, — a bitter cold
night," was the irrelevant commencement of
his defense. "You've all traveled trail, and
know what that stands for. Don't jump a
dog when he's down. You've only heard
one side. A whiter man than Jack Westondale never ate from the same pot nor stretched

blanket with you or me.   Last fall he gave
his whole clean-up, forty thousand, to Joe
Castrell, to buy in on Dominion.   To-day
he 'd be a millionaire.   But while he stayed
behind at Circle City, taking care of his partner with the scurvy, what does Castrell do?
Goes into McFarland's, jumps the limit, and
drops the whole sack.   Found him dead in
the snow the next day.   And poor Jack laying his plans to go out this winter to his wife
and the boy he 's never seen.   You 'll notice
he took exactly what his partner lost, — forty
thousand.   Well, he 's gone out; and what
are you going to do about it ? "

The Kid glanced round the circle of his
judges, noted the softening of their faces,
then raised his mug aloft.   " So a health to
the man on trail this night ; may his grub
hold out ; may his dogs keep their legs ; may
his matches never miss fire.   God prosper
him ; good luck go with him ; and " —

" Confusion to the Mounted Police! " cried
Bettles, to the crash of the empty cups.

THE PRIESTLY PREROGATIVE

This is the story of a man who did not appreciate his wife; also, of a woman who did him too great an honor when she gave herself to him. Incidentally, it concerns a Jesuit priest who had never been known to lie. He was an appurtenance, and a very necessary one, to the Yukon country; but the presence of the other two was merely accidental. They were specimens of the many strange waifs which ride the breast of a gold rush or come tailing along behind.

Edwin Bentham and Grace Bentham were waifs; they were also tailing along behind, for the Klondike rush of '97 had long since swept down the great river and subsided into the famine-stricken city of Dawson. When the Yukon shut up shop and went to sleep under a three-foot ice-sheet, this peripatetic couple found themselves at the Five Finger Rapids, with the City of Gold still a journey of many sleeps to the north.

Not a few cattle had been butchered at this

place in the fall of the year, and the offal
made a goodly heap. The three fellow *voyageurs* of Edwin Bentham and wife gazed
upon this deposit, did a little mental arithmetic,
caught a certain glimpse of a bonanza, and
decided to remain. And all winter they sold
sacks of bones and frozen hides to the fam-
ished dog-teams. It was a modest price they
asked, a dollar a pound, just as it came. Six
months later, when the sun came back and
the Yukon awoke, they buckled on their heavy
money-belts and journeyed back to the Southland, where they yet live and lie mightily
about the Klondike they never saw.

But Edwin Bentham — he was an indolent
fellow, and had he not been possessed of a
wife, would have gladly joined issues in the
dog-meat speculation. As it was, she played
upon his vanity, told him how great and
strong he was, how a man such as he certainly was could overcome all obstacles and
of a surety obtain the Golden Fleece. So he
squared his jaw, sold his share in the bones
and hides for a sled and one dog, and turned
his snowshoes to the north. Needless to state,
Grace Bentham's snowshoes never allowed
his tracks to grow cold. Nay, ere their tribu-

lations had seen three days, it was the man who followed in the rear, and the woman who broke trail in advance. Of course, if anybody hove in sight, the position was instantly reversed. Thus did his manhood remain virgin to the travelers who passed like ghosts on the silent trail. There are such men in this world.

How such a man and such a woman came to take each other for better and for worse is unimportant to this narrative. These things are familiar to us all, and those people who do them, or even question them too closely, are apt to lose a beautiful faith which is known as Eternal Fitness.

Edwin Bentham was a boy, thrust by mischance into a man's body, — a boy who could complacently pluck a butterfly, wing from wing, or cower in abject terror before a lean, nervy fellow, not half his size. He was a selfish cry-baby, hidden behind a man's mustache and stature, and glossed over with a skin-deep veneer of culture and conventionality. Yes; he was a clubman and a society man, — the sort that grace social functions and utter inanities with a charm and unction which are indescribable; the sort that talk big, and cry over a toothache; the sort that

put more hell into a woman's life by marrying
her than can the most graceless libertine that
ever browsed in forbidden pastures. We meet
these men every day, but we rarely know them
for what they are. Second to marrying them,
the best way to get this knowledge is to eat
out of the same pot and crawl under the same
blanket with them for — well, say a week ; no
greater margin is necessary.

To see Grace Bentham was to see a slender,
girlish creature ; to know her was to know a
soul which dwarfed one's own, yet retained all
the elements of the eternal feminine. This was
the woman who urged and encouraged her
husband in his Northland quest, who broke
trail for him when no one was looking, and
cried in secret over her weakling woman's body.

So journeyed this strangely assorted couple
down to old Fort Selkirk, then through fivescore miles of dismal wilderness to Stuart River.
And when the short day left them, and the
man lay down in the snow and blubbered, it
was the woman who lashed him to the sled,
bit her lips with the pain of her aching limbs,
and helped the dog haul him to Malemute
Kid's cabin. Malemute Kid was not at home,
but Meyers, the German trader, cooked great

moose-steaks and shook up a bed of fresh pine boughs.

Lake, Langham, and Parker were excited, and not unduly so when the cause was taken into account.

"Oh, Sandy! Say, can you tell a porter-house from a round? Come out and lend us a hand, anyway!" This appeal emanated from the cache, where Langham was vainly struggling with divers quarters of frozen moose.

"Don't you budge from those dishes!" commanded Parker.

"I say, Sandy — there's a good fellow — just run down to the Missouri Camp and borrow some cinnamon," begged Lake.

"Oh! oh! hurry up! Why don't" — But the crash of meat and boxes, in the cache, abruptly quenched this peremptory summons.

"Come now, Sandy; it won't take a minute to go down to the Missouri" —

"You leave him alone," interrupted Parker. "How am I to mix the biscuits if the table is n't cleared off?"

Sandy paused in indecision, till suddenly the fact that he was Langham's "man" dawned upon him. Then he apologetically threw down the greasy dishcloth, and went to his master's rescue.

These promising scions of wealthy progenitors had come to the Northland in search of laurels, with much money to burn, and a "man" apiece. Luckily for their souls, the other two men were up the White River in search of a mythical quartz-ledge ; so Sandy had to grin under the responsibility of three healthy masters, each of whom was possessed of peculiar cookery ideas. Twice that morning had a disruption of the whole camp been imminent, only averted by immense concessions from one or the other of these knights of the chafing-dish. But at last their mutual creation, a really dainty dinner, was completed. Then they sat down to a three-cornered game of "cut-throat," — a proceeding which did away with all *casus belli* for future hostilities, and permitted the victor to depart on a most important mission.

This fortune fell to Parker, who parted his hair in the middle, put on his mittens and bear-skin cap, and stepped over to Malemute Kid's cabin. And when he returned, it was in the company of Grace Bentham and Male-

mute Kid, — the former very sorry her husband
could not share with her their hospitality, for
he had gone up to look at the Henderson
Creek mines, and the latter still a trifle stiff
from breaking trail down the Stuart River.
Meyers had been asked, but had declined, being deeply engrossed in an experiment of
raising bread from hops.

Well, they could do without the husband;
but a woman — why, they had not seen one
all winter, and the presence of this one promised a new hegira in their lives. They were
college men and gentlemen, these three young
fellows, yearning for the flesh-pots they had
been so long denied. Probably Grace Bentham suffered from a similar hunger; at least,
it meant much to her, the first bright hour in
many weeks of darkness.

But that wonderful first course, which
claimed the versatile Lake for its parent, had
no sooner been served than there came a loud
knock at the door.

"Oh! Ah! Won't you come in, Mr. Bentham?" said Parker, who had stepped to see
who the newcomer might be.

"Is my wife here?" gruffly responded that
worthy.

"Why, yes. We left word with Mr. Meyers." Parker was exerting his most dulcet tones, inwardly wondering what the deuce it all meant. "Won't you come in? Expecting you at any moment, we reserved a place. And just in time for the first course, too."

"Come in, Edwin, dear," chirped Grace Bentham from her seat at the table.

Parker naturally stood aside.

"I want my wife," reiterated Bentham hoarsely, the intonation savoring disagreeably of ownership.

Parker gasped, was within an ace of driving his fist into the face of his boorish visitor, but held himself awkwardly in check. Everybody rose. Lake lost his head and caught himself on the verge of saying, "Must you go?"

Then began the farrago of leave-taking. "So nice of you" — "Awfully sorry" — "By Jove! how things did brighten" — "Really now, you" — "Thank you ever so much" — "Nice trip to Dawson" — etc.

In this wise the lamb was helped into her jacket and led to the slaughter. Then the door slammed, and they gazed woefully upon the deserted table.

"Damn!" Langham had suffered disadvantages in his early training, and his oaths were weak and monotonous. "Damn!" he repeated, vaguely conscious of the incompleteness and vainly struggling for a more virile term.

It is a clever woman who can fill out the many weak places in an inefficient man, by her own indomitability reinforce his vacillating nature, infuse her ambitious soul into his, and spur him on to great achievements. And it is indeed a very clever and tactful woman who can do all this, and do it so subtly that the man receives all the credit and believes in his inmost heart that everything is due to him and him alone.

This is what Grace Bentham proceeded to do. Arriving in Dawson with a few pounds of flour and several letters of introduction, she at once applied herself to the task of pushing her big baby to the fore. It was she who melted the stony heart and wrung credit from the rude barbarian who presided over the destiny of the P. C. Company; yet it was Edwin Bentham to whom the concession was ostensibly granted. It was she who dragged her baby up and down creeks, over benches and divides, and on a dozen wild stampedes; yet everybody remarked what an energetic fellow that Bentham was. It was she who studied maps, and catechised miners, and hammered geography and locations into his hollow head, till everybody marveled at his broad grasp of the country and knowledge of its conditions. Of course, they said the wife was a brick, and only a few wise ones appreciated and pitied her.

She did the work; he got the credit and reward. In the Northwest Territory a married woman cannot stake or record a creek, bench, or quartz claim; so Edwin Bentham went down to the Gold Commissioner and filed on Bench Claim 23, second tier, of French Hill. And when April came they were washing out a thousand dollars a day, with many, many such days in prospect.

At the base of French Hill lay Eldorado Creek, and on a creek claim stood the cabin of Clyde Wharton. At present he was not washing out a diurnal thousand dollars; but his dumps grew, shift by shift, and there would come a time when those dumps would pass through his sluice-boxes, depositing in the riffles, in the course of half a dozen days, several hundred thousand dollars. He often sat in that cabin, smoked his pipe, and dreamed beautiful little dreams, — dreams in which neither the dumps nor the half-ton of dust in the P. C. Company's big safe played a part.

And Grace Bentham, as she washed tin dishes in her hillside cabin, often glanced down into Eldorado Creek, and dreamed, — not of dumps nor dust, however. They met frequently, as the trail to the one claim crossed the other, and there is much to talk about in the Northland spring ; but never once, by the light of an eye nor the slip of a tongue, did they speak their hearts.

This is as it was at first. But one day Edwin Bentham was brutal. All boys are thus ; besides, being a French Hill king now, he began to think a great deal of himself and to forget all he owed to his wife. On this day, Wharton heard of it, and waylaid Grace Bentham, and talked wildly. This made her very happy, though she would not listen, and made him promise to not say such things again. Her hour had not come.

But the sun swept back on its northern

journey, the black of midnight changed to
the steely color of dawn, the snow slipped
away, the water dashed again over the glacial
drift, and the wash-up began. Day and night
the yellow clay and scraped bed-rock hurried
through the swift sluices, yielding up its ransom to the strong men from the Southland.
And in that time of tumult came Grace Bentham's hour.

To all of us such hours at some time come,
— that is, to us who are not too phlegmatic.
Some people are good, not from inherent love
of virtue, but from sheer laziness. Those of
us who know weak moments may understand.

Edwin Bentham was weighing dust over
the bar of the saloon at the Forks — alto-
gether too much of his dust went over that
pine board —when his wife came down the
hill and slipped into Clyde Wharton's cabin.
Wharton was not expecting her, but that
did not alter the case. And much subsequent
misery and idle waiting might have been
avoided, had not Father Roubeau seen this
and turned aside from the main creek trail.

"My child " —
" Hold on, Father Roubeau! Though

I'm not of your faith, I respect you; but you can't come in between this woman and me!"

"You know what you are doing?"

"Know! Were you God Almighty, ready to fling me into eternal fire, I'd bank my will against yours in this matter."

Wharton had placed Grace on a stool and stood belligerently before her.

"You sit down on that chair and keep quiet," he continued, addressing the Jesuit. "I'll take my innings now. You can have yours after."

Father Roubeau bowed courteously and obeyed. He was an easy-going man and had learned to bide his time. Wharton pulled a stool alongside the woman's, smothering her hand in his.

"Then you do care for me, and will take me away?"

Her face seemed to reflect the peace of this man, against whom she might draw close for shelter.

"Dear, don't you remember what I said before? Of course I" —

"But how can you? — the wash-up?"

"Do you think that worries? Anyway,

I'll give the job to Father Roubeau, here. I can trust him to safely bank the dust with the company."

" To think of it! — I'll never see him again."

" A blessing!"

" And to go — Oh, Clyde, I can't! I can't!"

" There, there; of course you can. Just let me plan it. You see, as soon as we get a few traps together, we'll start, and " —

" Suppose he comes back?"

" I'll break every " —

" No, no! No fighting, Clyde! Promise me that."

" All right! I'll just tell the men to throw him off the claim. They've seen how he's treated you, and haven't much love for him."

" You mustn't do that. You mustn't hurt him."

" What then? Let him come right in here and take you away before my eyes?"

" No-o," she half whispered, stroking his hand softly.

" Then let me run it, and don't worry. I'll see he doesn't get hurt. Precious lot he cared whether you got hurt or not! We won't go back to Dawson. I'll send word down for a couple of the boys to outfit and pole a boat up the Yukon. We'll cross the divide and raft down the Indian River to meet them. Then " —

" And then ? "

Her head was on his shoulder. Their voices sank to softer cadences, each word a caress. The Jesuit fidgeted nervously.

" And then ? " she repeated.

" Why, we'll pole up, and up, and up, and portage the White Horse Rapids and the Box Cañon."

" Yes ? "

" And the Sixty-Mile River; then the lakes, Chilcoot, Dyea, and Salt Water."

" But, dear, I can't pole a boat."

" You little goose ! I'll get Sitka Charley; he knows all the good water and best camps, and he is the best traveler I ever met, if he is an Indian. All you'll have to do, is to sit in the middle of the boat, and sing songs, and play Cleopatra, and fight — no, we're in luck ; too early for mosquitoes."

" And then, O my Antony ? "

" And then a steamer, San Francisco, and the world ! Never to come back to this cursed hole again. Think of it! The world, and ours to choose from! I'll sell out. Why, we're rich! The Waldworth Syndicate will give me half a million for what's left in the ground, and I've got twice as much in the dumps and with the P. C. Company. We'll go to the Fair in Paris in 1900. We'll go to Jerusalem, if you say so. We'll buy an Italian palace, and you can play Cleopatra to your heart's content. No, you shall be Lucretia, Acte, or anybody your little heart sees fit to become. But you must n't, you really must n't " —

" The wife of Cæsar shall be above reproach."

" Of course, but " —

" But I won't be your wife, will I, dear ? "

" I did n't mean that."

" But you'll love me just as much, and never even think — oh ! I know you'll be like other men ; you'll grow tired, and — and " —

" How can you ? I " —

" Promise me."

" Yes, yes ; I do promise."

" You say it so easily, dear ; but how do you know ? — or I know ? I have so little

to give, yet it is so much. Oh, Clyde! promise
me you won't?"

"There, there! You mustn't begin to
doubt already. Till death do us part, you
know."

"Think! I once said that to — to him,
and now?"

"And now, little sweetheart, you're not
to bother about such things any more. Of
course, I never, never will, and " —

And for the first time, lips trembled against
lips. Father Roubeau had been watching the
main trail through the window, but could
stand the strain no longer. He cleared his
throat and turned around.

"Your turn now, Father!" Wharton's
face was flushed with the fire of his first em-
brace. There was an exultant ring to his
voice as he abdicated in the other's favor.
He had no doubt as to the result. Neither
had Grace, for a smile played about her
mouth as she faced the priest.

"My child," he began, "my heart bleeds
for you. It is a pretty dream, but it cannot
be."

"And why, Father? I have said yes."

"You knew not what you did. You did

not think of the oath you took, before your God, to that man who is your husband. It remains for me to make you realize the sanctity of such a pledge."

"And if I do realize, and yet refuse?"

"Then God"—

"Which God? My husband has a God which I care not to worship. There must be many such."

"Child! unsay those words! Ah! you do not mean them. I understand. I, too, have had such moments." For an instant he was back in his native France, and a wistful, sad-eyed face came as a mist between him and the woman before him.

"Then, Father, has my God forsaken me? I am not wicked above women. My misery with him has been great. Why should it be greater? Why shall I not grasp at happiness? I cannot, will not, go back to him!"

"Rather is your God forsaken. Return. Throw your burden upon Him, and the darkness shall be lifted. Oh, my child"—

"No; it is useless; I have made my bed and so shall I lie. I will go on. And if God punishes me, I shall bear it somehow. You do not understand. You are not a woman."

" My mother was a woman."

" But " —

" And Christ was born of woman."

She did not answer. A silence fell. Wharton pulled his mustache impatiently and kept an eye on the trail. Grace leaned her elbow on the table, her face set with resolve. The smile had died away. Father Roubeau shifted his ground.

" You have children?"

" At one time I wished — but now — no. And I am thankful."

" And a mother?"

" Yes."

" She loves you?"

" Yes." Her replies were whispers.

" And a brother? — no matter, he is a man. But a sister?"

Her head drooped a quavering yes.

" Younger? Very much?"

" Seven years."

" And you have thought well about this matter? About them? About your mother? And your sister? She stands on the threshold of her woman's life, and this wildness of yours may mean much to her. Could you go before her, look upon her fresh young face, hold her hand in yours, or touch your cheek to hers?"

To his words, her brain formed vivid images, till she cried out, "Don't! don't!" and shrank away as do the wolf-dogs from the lash.

"But you must face all this; and better it is to do it now."

In his eyes, which she could not see, there was a great compassion, but his face, tense and quivering, showed no relenting. She raised her head from the table, forced back the tears, struggled for control.

"I shall go away. They will never see me, and come to forget me. I shall be to them as dead. And — and I will go with Clyde — to-day."

It seemed final. Wharton stepped forward, but the priest waved him back.

"You have wished for children?"

A silent yes.

"And prayed for them?"

"Often."

"And have you thought, if you should have children?" Father Roubeau's eyes rested for a moment on the man by the window.

A quick light shot across her face. Then

the full import dawned upon her. She raised her hand appealingly, but he went on.

" Can you picture an innocent babe in your arms ? A boy ? The world is not so hard upon a girl. Why, your very breast would turn to gall ! And you could be proud and happy of your boy, as you looked on other children ? " —

" Oh, have pity ! Hush ! "

" A scapegoat " —

" Don't ! don't ! I will go back ! " She was at his feet.

" A child to grow up with no thought of evil, and one day the world to fling a tender name in his face ! "

" O my God ! my God ! "

She groveled on the floor. The priest sighed and raised her to her feet. Wharton pressed forward, but she motioned him away.

" Don't come near me, Clyde ! I am going back ! " The tears were coursing pitifully down her face, but she made no effort to wipe them away.

" After all this ? You cannot ! I will not let you ! "

" Don't touch me ! " She shivered and drew back.

"I will! You are mine! Do you hear? You are mine!" Then he whirled upon the priest. "Oh, what a fool I was to ever let you wag your silly tongue! Thank your God you are not a common man, for I'd — But the priestly prerogative must be exercised, eh? Well, you have exercised it. Now get out of my house, or I'll forget who and what you are!"

Father Roubeau bowed, took her hand, and started for the door. But Wharton cut them off.

"Grace! You said you loved me?"

"I did."

"And you do now?"

"I do."

"Say it again."

"I do love you, Clyde; I do."

"There, you priest!" he cried. "You have heard it, and with those words on her lips you would send her back to live a lie and a hell with that man?"

But Father Roubeau whisked the woman into the inner room and closed the door. "No words!" he whispered to Wharton, as he struck a casual posture on a stool. "Remember, for her sake," he added.

The room echoed to a rough knock at the door; then the latch raised and Edwin Bentham stepped in.

"Seen anything of my wife?" he asked, as soon as salutations had been exchanged.

Two heads nodded negatively.

"I saw her tracks down from the cabin," he continued tentatively, "and they broke off, just opposite here, on the main trail."

His listeners looked bored.

"And I — I thought" —

"She was here!" thundered Wharton.

The priest silenced him with a look. "Did you see her tracks leading up to this cabin, my son?" Wily Father Roubeau — he had taken good care to obliterate them as he came up the same path an hour before.

"I didn't stop to look, I" — His eyes rested suspiciously on the door to the other room, then interrogated the priest. The latter shook his head; but the doubt seemed to linger.

Father Roubeau breathed a swift, silent prayer, and rose to his feet. "If you doubt me, why" — He made as though to open the door.

A priest could not lie. Edwin Bentham

had heard this often, and believed it. "Of course not, Father," he interposed hurriedly. "I was only wondering where my wife had gone, and thought maybe — I guess she's up at Mrs. Stanton's on French Gulch. Nice weather, isn't it? Heard the news? Flour's gone down to forty dollars a hundred, and they say the *che-cha-quas* are flocking down the river in droves. But I must be going; so good-by."

The door slammed, and from the window they watched him take his quest up French Gulch.

A few weeks later, just after the June high-water, two men shot a canoe into midstream and made fast to a derelict pine. This tightened the painter and jerked the frail craft along as would a tow-boat. Father Roubeau had been directed to leave the Upper Country and return to his swarthy children at Minook. The white men had come among them, and they were devoting too little time to fishing, and too much to a certain deity whose transient habitat was in countless black bottles. Malemute Kid also had business in the Lower Country, so they journeyed together.

But one, in all the Northland, knew the man Paul Roubeau, and that man was Malemute Kid. Before him alone did the priest cast off the sacerdotal garb and stand naked. And why not? These two men knew each other. Had they not shared the last morsel of fish, the last pinch of tobacco, the last and inmost thought, on the barren stretches of Bering Sea, in the heart-breaking mazes of the Great Delta, on the terrible winter journey from Point Barrow to the Porcupine?

Father Roubeau puffed heavily at his trail-worn pipe, and gazed on the red-disked sun, poised sombrely on the edge of the northern horizon. Malemute Kid wound up his watch. It was midnight.

"Cheer up, old man!" The Kid was evidently gathering up a broken thread. "God surely will forgive such a lie. Let me give you the word of a man who strikes a true note : —

"'If She have spoken a word, remember thy lips are sealed,
And the brand of the Dog is upon him by whom is the secret revealed.
If there be trouble to Herward, and a lie of the blackest can clear,
Lie, while thy lips can move or a man is alive to hear.'"

Father Roubeau removed his pipe and reflected. " The man speaks true, but my soul is not vexed with that. The lie and the penance stand with God ; but — but " —

" What then ? Your hands are clean."

" Not so. Kid, I have thought much, and yet the thing remains. I knew, and I made her go back."

The clear note of a robin rang out from the wooded bank, a partridge drummed the call in the distance, a moose lunged noisily in an eddy, but the twain smoked on in silence.

THE WISDOM OF THE TRAIL

SITKA CHARLEY had achieved the impossible. Other Indians might have known as much of the wisdom of the trail as did he; but he alone knew the white man's wisdom, the honor of the trail, and the law. But these things had not come to him in a day. The aboriginal mind is slow to generalize, and many facts, repeated often, are required to compass an understanding. Sitka Charley, from boyhood, had been thrown continually with white men, and as a man he had elected to cast his fortunes with them, expatriating himself, once and for all, from his own people. Even then, respecting, almost venerating their power, and pondering over it, he had yet to divine its secret essence — the honor and the law. And it was only by the cumulative evidence of years that he had finally come to understand. Being an alien, when he did know he knew it better than the white man himself; being an Indian, he had achieved the impossible.

And of these things had been bred a certain contempt for his own people, — a contempt which he had made it a custom to conceal, but which now burst forth in a polyglot whirlwind of curses upon the heads of Kah-Chucte and Gowhee. They cringed before him like a brace of snarling wolf-dogs, too cowardly to spring, too wolfish to cover their fangs. They were not handsome creatures. Neither was Sitka Charley. All three were frightful-looking. There was no flesh to their faces; their cheek bones were massed with hideous scabs which had cracked and frozen alternately under the intense frost; while their eyes burned luridly with the light which is born of desperation and hunger. Men so situated, beyond the pale of the honor and the law, are not to be trusted. Sitka Charley knew this; and this was why he had forced them to abandon their rifles with the rest of the camp outfit ten days before. His rifle and Captain Eppingwell's were the only ones that remained.

"Come, get a fire started," he commanded, drawing out the precious match box with its attendant strips of dry birch bark.

The two Indians fell sullenly to the task

of gathering dead branches and underwood.
They were weak, and paused often, catching
themselves, in the act of stooping, with giddy
motions, or staggering to the centre of opera-
tions with their knees shaking like castanets.
After each trip they rested for a moment, as
though sick and deadly weary. At times
their eyes took on the patient stoicism of
dumb suffering ; and again the ego seemed
almost bursting forth with its wild cry, " I,
I, I want to exist ! " — the dominant note of
the whole living universe.

A light breath of air blew from the
south, nipping the exposed portions of their
bodies and driving the frost, in needles of
fire, through fur and flesh to the bones. So,
when the fire had grown lusty and thawed a
damp circle in the snow about it, Sitka Charley forced his reluctant comrades to lend a
hand in pitching a fly. It was a primitive affair, — merely a blanket, stretched parallel
with the fire and to windward of it, at an angle
of perhaps forty-five degrees. This shut out
the chill wind, and threw the heat backward
and down upon those who were to huddle in
its shelter. Then a layer of green spruce
boughs was spread, that their bodies might

not come in contact with the snow. When this task was completed, Kah-Chucte and Gowhee proceeded to take care of their feet. Their ice-bound moccasins were sadly worn by much travel, and the sharp ice of the river jams had cut them to rags. Their Siwash socks were similarly conditioned, and when these had been thawed and removed, the dead-white tips of the toes, in the various stages of mortification, told their simple tale of the trail.

Leaving the two to the drying of their footgear, Sitka Charley turned back over the course he had come. He, too, had a mighty longing to sit by the fire and tend his complaining flesh, but the honor and the law forbade. He toiled painfully over the frozen field, each step a protest, every muscle in revolt. Several times, where the open water between the jams had recently crusted, he was forced to miserably accelerate his movements as the fragile footing swayed and threatened beneath him. In such places death was quick and easy; but it was not his desire to endure no more.

His deepening anxiety vanished as two Indians dragged into view round a bend in the river. They staggered and panted like men under heavy burdens ; yet the packs on their backs were a matter of but few pounds. He questioned them eagerly, and their replies seemed to relieve him. He hurried on. Next came two white men, supporting between them a woman. They also behaved as though drunken, and their limbs shook with weakness. But the woman leaned lightly upon them, choosing to carry herself forward with her own strength. At sight of her, a flash of joy cast its fleeting light across Sitka Charley's face. He cherished a very great regard for Mrs. Eppingwell. He had seen many white women, but this was the first to travel the trail with him. When Captain Eppingwell proposed the hazardous undertaking and made him an offer for his services, he had shaken his head gravely; for it was an unknown journey through the dismal vastnesses of the Northland, and he knew it to be of the kind that try to the uttermost the souls of men. But when he learned that the Captain's wife was to accompany them, he had refused flatly to have anything further to do with it. Had it been a woman of his own race he would have harbored no objec-

tions ; but these women of the Southland —
no, no, they were too soft, too tender, for
such enterprises.

Sitka Charley did not know this kind of
woman.   Five minutes before, he did not
even dream of taking charge of the expedition ; but when she came to him with her
wonderful smile and her straight clean English, and talked to the point, without plead-
ing or persuading, he had incontinently
yielded.   Had there been a softness and appeal to mercy in the eyes, a tremble to the
voice, a taking advantage of sex, he would
have stiffened to steel ; instead her clear-
searching eyes and clear-ringing voice, her
utter frankness and tacit assumption of equal-
ity, had robbed him of his reason.   He felt,
then, that this was a new breed of woman ;
and ere they had been trail-mates for many
days, he knew why the sons of such women
mastered the land and the sea, and why the
sons of his own womankind could not prevail
against them.   *Tender and soft!*   Day after
day he watched her, muscle-weary, exhausted,
indomitable, and the words beat in upon him
in a perennial refrain.   *Tender and soft!*
He knew her feet had been born to easy

paths and sunny lands, strangers to the moccasined pain of the North, unkissed by the
chill lips of the frost, and he watched and
marveled at them twinkling ever through the
weary day.

She had always a smile and a word of cheer,
from which not even the meanest packer
was excluded.   As the way grew darker
she seemed to stiffen and gather greater
strength, and when Kah-Chucte and Gowhee,
who had bragged that they knew every land-
mark of the way as a child did the skin-bales
of the tepee, acknowledged that they knew
not where they were, it was she who raised a
forgiving voice amid the curses of the men.
She had sung to them that night, till they
felt the weariness fall from them and were
ready to face the future with fresh hope.
And when the food failed and each scant
stint was measured jealously, she it was who
rebelled against the machinations of her husband and Sitka Charley, and demanded and
received a share neither greater nor less than
that of the others.

Sitka Charley was proud to know this woman. A new richness, a greater breadth, had
come into his life with her presence. Hith-

erto he had been his own mentor, had turned
to right or left at no man's beck; he had
moulded himself according to his own dic-
tates, nourished his manhood regardless of
all save his own opinion. For the first time
he had felt a call from without for the best
that was in him. Just a glance of apprecia-
tion from the clear-searching eyes, a word of
thanks from the clear-ringing voice, just a
slight wreathing of the lips in the wonderful
smile, and he walked with the gods for hours
to come. It was a new stimulant to his manhood; for the first time he thrilled with a
conscious pride in his wisdom of the trail;
and between the twain they ever lifted the
sinking hearts of their comrades.

The faces of the two men and the woman
brightened as they saw him, for after all he
was the staff they leaned upon. But Sitka
Charley, rigid as was his wont, concealing
pain and pleasure impartially beneath an iron
exterior, asked them the welfare of the rest,
told the distance to the fire, and continued on
the back-trip. Next he met a single Indian,
unburdened, limping, lips compressed, and
eyes set with the pain of a foot in which the

quick fought a losing battle with the dead. All possible care had been taken of him, but in the last extremity the weak and unfortunate must perish, and Sitka Charley deemed his days to be few. The man could not keep up for long, so he gave him rough cheering words. After that came two more Indians, to whom he had allotted the task of helping along Joe, the third white man of the party. They had deserted him. Sitka Charley saw at a glance the lurking spring in their bodies, and knew they had at last cast off his mastery. So he was not taken unawares when he ordered them back in quest of their abandoned charge, and saw the gleam of the hunting-knives that they drew from the sheaths. A pitiful spectacle, three weak men lifting their puny strength in the face of the mighty vastness; but the two recoiled under the fierce rifle-blows of the one, and returned like beaten dogs to the leash. Two hours later, with Joe reeling between them and Sitka Charley bringing up the rear, they came to the fire, where the remainder of the expedition crouched in the shelter of the fly.

" A few words, my comrades, before we sleep," Sitka Charley said, after they had de-

voured their slim rations of unleavened bread.
He was speaking to the Indians, in their own
tongue, having already given the import to
the whites. " A few words, my comrades,
for your own good, that ye may yet per-
chance live. I shall give you the law ; on
his own head be the death of him that breaks
it. We have passed the Hills of Silence, and
we now travel the head-reaches of the Stuart.
It may be one sleep, it may be several, it may
be many sleeps, but in time we shall come
among the Men of the Yukon, who have
much grub. It were well that we look to the
law. To-day, Kah-Chucte and Gowhee, whom
I commanded to break trail, forgot they were
men, and like frightened children ran away.
True, they forgot ; so let us forget. But
hereafter let them remember. If it should
happen they do not " — He touched his rifle
carelessly, grimly. " To-morrow they shall
carry the flour and see that the white man
Joe lies not down by the trail. The cups of
flour are counted ; should so much as an
ounce be wanting at nightfall — Do ye understand ? To-day there were others that
forgot. Moose-Head and Three-Salmon left
the white man Joe to lie in the snow. Let

them forget no more. With the light of day shall they go forth and break trail. Ye have heard the law. Look well, lest ye break it."

Sitka Charley found it beyond him to keep the line close up. From Moose-Head and Three-Salmon, who broke trail in advance, to Kah-Chucte, Gowhee, and Joe, it straggled out over a mile. Each staggered, fell, or rested, as he saw fit. The line of march was a progression through a chain of irregular halts. Each drew upon the last remnant of his strength and stumbled onward till it was expended, but in some miraculous way there was always another last remnant. Each time a man fell, it was with the firm belief that he would rise no more ; yet he did rise, and again, and again. The flesh yielded, the will conquered ; but each triumph was a tragedy. The Indian with the frozen foot, no longer erect, crawled forward on hand and knee. He rarely rested, for he knew the penalty exacted by the frost. Even Mrs. Eppingwell's lips were at last set in a stony smile, and her eyes, seeing, saw not. Often, she stopped, pressing a mittened hand to her heart, gasping and dizzy.

Joe, the white man, had passed beyond the stage of suffering. He no longer begged to be let alone, prayed to die; but was soothed and content under the anodyne of delirium. Kah-Chucte and Gowhee dragged him on roughly, venting upon him many a savage glance or blow. To them it was the acme of injustice. Their hearts were bitter with hate, heavy with fear. Why should they cumber their strength with his weakness? To do so, meant death; not to do so — and they remembered the law of Sitka Charley, and the rifle.

Joe fell with greater frequency as the daylight waned, and so hard was he to raise that they dropped farther and farther behind. Sometimes all three pitched into the snow, so weak had the Indians become. Yet on their backs was life, and strength, and warmth. Within the flour-sacks were all the potentialities of existence. They could not but think of this, and it was not strange, that which came to pass. They had fallen by the side of a great timber-jam where a thousand cords of firewood waited the match. Near by was an air hole through the ice. Kah-Chucte looked on the wood and the water, as did Gowhee; then they looked on each other. Never

a word was spoken.   Gowhee struck a fire;
Kah-Chucte filled a tin cup with water and
heated it; Joe babbled of things in another
land, in a tongue they did not understand.
They mixed flour with the warm water till it
was a thin paste, and of this they drank many
cups.   They did not offer any to Joe; but
he did not mind.   He did not mind anything,
not even his moccasins, which scorched and
smoked among the coals.

A crystal mist of snow fell about them,
softly, caressingly, wrapping them in clinging
robes of white.   And their feet would have
yet trod many trails had not destiny brushed
the clouds aside and cleared the air.   Nay, ten
minutes' delay would have been salvation.
Sitka Charley, looking back, saw the pillared
smoke of their fire, and guessed.   And he
looked ahead at those who were faithful, and
at Mrs. Eppingwell.

" So, my good comrades, ye have again forgotten that you were men?   Good.   Very good.
There will be fewer bellies to feed."

Sitka Charley retied the flour as he spoke,
strapping the pack to the one on his own back.
He kicked Joe till the pain broke through the

poor devil's bliss and brought him doddering to his feet. Then he shoved him out upon the trail and started him on his way. The two Indians attempted to slip off.

"Hold, Gowhee! And thou, too, Kah-Chucte! Hath the flour given such strength to thy legs that they may outrun the swift-winged lead? Think not to cheat the law. Be men for the last time, and be content that ye die full-stomached. Come, step up, back to the timber, shoulder to shoulder. Come!"

The two men obeyed, quietly, without fear; for it is the future which presses upon the man, not the present.

"Thou, Gowhee, hast a wife and children and a deer-skin lodge in the Chippewyan. What is thy will in the matter?"

"Give thou her of the goods which are mine by the word of the Captain — the blankets, the beads, the tobacco, the box which makes strange sounds after the manner of the white men. Say that I did die on the trail, but say not how."

"And thou, Kah-Chucte, who hast nor wife nor child?"

"Mine is a sister, the wife of the Factor at Koshim. He beats her, and she is not happy.

"Are ye content to die by the law?"

Give thou her the goods which are mine by the contract, and tell her it were well she go back to her own people. Shouldst thou meet the man, and be so minded, it were a good deed that he should die. He beats her, and she is afraid."

"Are ye content to die by the law?"

"We are."

"Then good-by, my good comrades. May ye sit by the well-filled pot, in warm lodges, ere the day is done."

As he spoke, he raised his rifle, and many echoes broke the silence. Hardly had they died away, when other rifles spoke in the distance. Sitka Charley started. There had been more than one shot, yet there was but one other rifle in the party. He gave a fleeting glance at the men who lay so quietly, smiled viciously at the wisdom of the trail, and hurried on to meet the Men of the Yukon.

THE WIFE OF A KING

I

ONCE, when the Northland was very young, the social and civic virtues were remarkable alike for their paucity and their simplicity. When the burden of domestic duties grew grievous, and the fireside mood expanded to a constant protest against its bleak loneliness, the adventurers from the Southland, in lieu of better, paid the stipulated prices and took unto themselves native wives. It was a foretaste of Paradise to the women, for it must be confessed that the white rovers gave far better care and treatment to them than did their Indian copartners. Of course, the white men themselves were satisfied with such deals, as were also the Indian men for that matter. Having sold their daughters and sisters for cotton blankets and obsolete rifles, and traded their warm furs for flimsy calico and bad whiskey, the sons of the soil promptly and cheerfully succumbed to quick consumption and other swift diseases correlated with the blessings of a superior civilization.

It was in these days of Arcadian simplicity
that Cal Galbraith journeyed through the
land and fell sick on the Lower River. It
was a refreshing advent in the lives of the
good Sisters of the Holy Cross, who gave him
shelter and medicine; though they little
dreamed of the hot elixir infused into his
veins by the touch of their soft hands and
their gentle ministrations. Cal Galbraith became troubled with strange thoughts, which
clamored for attention till he laid eyes on the
Mission girl, Madeline. Yet he gave no sign,
biding his time patiently. He strengthened
with the coming spring, and when the sun
rode the heavens in a golden circle, and the
joy and throb of life were in all the land,
he gathered his still weak body together and
departed.

Now Madeline, the Mission girl, was an or-
phan. Her white father had failed to give a
bald-faced grizzly the trail one day, and had
died quickly. Then her Indian mother, having no man to fill the winter cache, had tried
the hazardous experiment of waiting till the
salmon-run on fifty pounds of flour and half
as many of bacon. After that the baby,
Chook-ra, went to live with the good Sisters,

and to be thenceforth known by another name.

But Madeline still had kinsfolk, the nearest being a dissolute uncle who outraged his vitals with inordinate quantities of the white man's whiskey. He strove daily to walk with the gods, and incidentally his feet sought shorter trails to the grave. When sober he suffered exquisite torture. He had no conscience. To this ancient vagabond Cal Galbraith duly presented himself, and they consumed many words and much tobacco in the conversation that followed. Promises were also made; and in the end the old heathen took a few pounds of dried salmon and his birch-bark canoe, and paddled away to the Mission of the Holy Cross.

It is not given the world to know what promises he made and what lies he told, — the Sisters never gossip; but when he returned, upon his swarthy chest there was a brass crucifix, and in his canoe his niece Madeline. That night there was a grand wedding and a *potlach*; so that for two days to follow there was no fishing done by the village. But in the morning Madeline shook the dust of the Lower River from her moccasins, and with her husband, in a poling-boat, went to live on the Upper River in a place known as the Lower Country. And in the years which followed she was a good wife, sharing her husband's hardships and cooking his food. And she kept him in straight trails, till he learned to save his dust and to work mightily. In the end, he struck it rich, and built a cabin in Circle City; and his happiness was such that men who came to visit him in his home circle became restless at the sight of it and envied him greatly.

But the Northland began to mature, and social amenities to make their appearance. Hitherto, the Southland had sent forth its sons; but it now belched forth a new exodus, this time of its daughters. Sisters and wives they were not; but they did not fail to put new ideas in the heads of the men, and to elevate the tone of things in ways peculiarly their own. No more did the squaws gather at the dances, go roaring down the centre in the good, old Virginia reels, or make merry with jolly "Dan Tucker." They fell back on their native stoicism, and uncomplainingly watched the rule of their white sisters from the cabins.

Then another exodus came over the mountains from the prolific Southland. This time it was of women that became mighty in the land. Their word was law; their law was steel. They frowned upon the Indian wives, while the other women became mild and walked humbly. There were cowards who became ashamed of their ancient covenants with the daughters of the soil, who looked with a new distaste upon their dark-skinned children; but there were also others — men — who remained true and proud of their aboriginal vows. When it became the fashion to divorce the native wives, Cal Galbraith retained his manhood, and in so doing felt the heavy hand of the women who had come last, knew least, but who ruled the land.

One day, the Upper Country, which lies far above Circle City, was pronounced rich. Dog-teams carried the news to Salt Water; golden argosies freighted the lure across the North Pacific; wires and cables sang with the tidings; and the world heard for the first time of the Klondike River and the Yukon Country.

Cal Galbraith had lived the years quietly.

He had been a good husband to Madeline, and she had blessed him. But somehow discontent fell upon him; he felt vague yearnings for his own kind, for the life he had been shut out from, — a general sort of desire, which men sometimes feel, to break out and taste the prime of living. Besides, there drifted down the river wild rumors of the wonderful Eldorado, glowing descriptions of the city of logs and tents, and ludicrous accounts of the *che-cha-quas* who had rushed in and were stampeding the whole country. Circle City was dead. The world had moved on up river and become a new and most marvelous world.

Cal Galbraith grew restless on the edge of things, and wished to see with his own eyes. So, after the wash-up, he weighed in a couple of hundred pounds of dust on the Company's big scales, and took a draft for the same on Dawson. Then he put Tom Dixon in charge of his mines, kissed Madeline goodby, promised to be back before the first mushice ran, and took passage on an up-river steamer.

Madeline waited, — waited through all the three months of daylight. She fed the dogs, gave much of her time to young Cal, watched the short summer fade away and the sun begin its long journey to the south. And she prayed much in the manner of the Sisters of the Holy Cross. The fall came, and with it there was mush-ice on the Yukon, and Circle City kings returning to the winter's work at their mines, but no Cal Galbraith. Tom Dixon received a letter, however, for his men sledded up her winter's supply of dry pine. The Company received a letter, for its dogteams filled her cache with their best provisions, and she was told that her credit was limitless.

Through all the ages man has been held the chief instigator of the woes of woman; but in this case the men held their tongues and swore harshly at one of their number who was away, while the women failed utterly to emulate them. So, without needless delay, Madeline heard strange tales of Cal Galbraith's doings; also, of a certain Greek dancer who played with men as children did with bubbles. Now Madeline was an Indian woman, and further, she had no woman friend to whom to go for wise counsel. She prayed and planned by turns, and that night, being quick of resolve and action, she harnessed the dogs, and with young Cal securely lashed to the sled, stole away.

Though the Yukon still ran free, the eddy-ice was growing, and each day saw the river dwindling to a slushy thread. Save him who has done the like, no man may know what she endured in traveling a hundred miles on the rim-ice; nor may they understand the toil and hardship of breaking the two hundred miles of packed ice which remained after the river froze for good. But Madeline was an Indian woman, so she did these things, and one night there came a knock at Malemute Kid's door. Thereat he fed a team of starving dogs, put a healthy youngster to bed, and turned his attention to an exhausted woman. He removed her ice-bound moccasins while he listened to her tale, and stuck the point of his knife into her feet that he might see how far they were frozen.

Despite his tremendous virility, Malemute Kid was possessed of a softer, womanly element, which could win the confidence of a snarling wolf-dog or draw confessions from the most wintry heart. Nor did he seek them. Hearts opened to him as spontaneously as flowers to the sun. Even the priest, Father Roubeau, had been known to confess to him, while the men and women of the Northland were ever knocking at his door, — a door from which the latch-string hung always out. To Madeline, he could do no wrong, make no mistake. She had known him from the time she first cast her lot among the people of her father's race; and to her half-barbaric mind it seemed that in him was centred the wisdom of the ages, that between his vision and the future there could be no intervening veil.

There were false ideals in the land. The social strictures of Dawson were not synonymous with those of the previous era, and the swift maturity of the Northland involved much wrong. Malemute Kid was aware of this, and he had Cal Galbraith's measure accurately. He knew a hasty word was the father of much evil; besides, he was minded to teach a great lesson and bring shame upon the man. So Stanley Prince, the young mining expert, was called into the conference the following night, as was also Lucky Jack Harrington and his violin. That same night, Bettles, who owed a great debt to Malemute

Kid, harnessed up Cal Galbraith's dogs, lashed Cal Galbraith, junior, to the sled, and slipped away in the dark for Stuart River.

II

"So; one — two — three, one — two — three. Now reverse! No, no! Start up again, Jack. See — this way." Prince executed the movement as one should who has led the cotillion.

"Now; one — two — three, one — two — three. Reverse! Ah! that's better. Try it again. I say, you know, you must n't look at your feet. One — two — three, one — two — three. Shorter steps! You are not hanging to the gee-pole just now. Try it over. There! that's the way. One — two — three, one — two — three."

Round and round went Prince and Madeline in an interminable waltz. The table and stools had been shoved over against the wall to increase the room. Malemute Kid sat on the bunk, chin to knees, greatly interested. Jack Harrington sat beside him, scraping away on his violin and following the dancers.

It was a unique situation, the undertaking

of these three men with the woman. The most pathetic part, perhaps, was the business-like way in which they went about it. No athlete was ever trained more rigidly for a coming contest, nor wolf-dog for the harness, than was she. But they had good material, for Madeline, unlike most women of her race, in her childhood had escaped the carrying of heavy burdens and the toil of the trail. Besides, she was a clean-limbed, willowy creature, possessed of much grace which had not hitherto been realized. It was this grace which the men strove to bring out and knock into shape.

"Trouble with her she learned to dance all wrong," Prince remarked to the bunk, after having deposited his breathless pupil on the table. "She's quick at picking up; yet I could do better had she never danced a step. But say, Kid, I can't understand this." Prince imitated a peculiar movement of the shoulders and head, — a weakness Madeline suffered from in walking.

"Lucky for her she was raised in the Mission," Malemute Kid answered. "Packing, you know, — the head-strap. Other Indian women have it bad, but she didn't do any packing till after she married, and then only at first. Saw hard lines with that husband of hers. They went through the Forty Mile famine together."

"But can we break it?"

"Don't know. Perhaps long walks with her trainers will make the riffle. Anyway, they'll take it out some, won't they, Madeline?"

The girl nodded assent. If Malemute Kid, who knew all things, said so, why, it was so. That was all there was about it.

She had come over to them, anxious to begin again. Harrington surveyed her in quest of her points, much in the same manner men do horses. It certainly was not disappointing, for he asked with sudden interest, "What did that beggarly uncle of yours get anyway?"

"One rifle, one blanket, twenty bottles of *hooch*. Rifle broke." She said this last scornfully, as though disgusted at how low her maiden-value had been rated.

She spoke fair English, with many peculiarities of her husband's speech, but there was still perceptible the Indian accent, the traditional groping after strange gutturals.

Even this her instructors had taken in hand, and with no small success, too.

At the next intermission Prince discovered a new predicament.

"I say, Kid," he said, "we're wrong, all wrong. She can't learn in moccasins. Put her feet into slippers, and then on to that waxed floor — phew!"

Madeline raised a foot and regarded her shapeless house-moccasin dubiously. In previous winters, both at Circle City and Forty Mile, she had danced many a night away with similar footgear, and there had been nothing the matter. But now — well, if there was anything wrong it was for Malemute Kid to know, not her.

But Malemute Kid did know, and he had a good eye for measures; so he put on his cap and mittens and went down the hill to pay Mrs. Eppingwell a call. Her husband, Clove Eppingwell, was prominent in the community as one of the great Government officials. The Kid had noted her slender little foot one night, at the Governor's Ball. And as he also knew her to be as sensible as she was pretty, it was no task to ask of her a certain small favor.

On his return, Madeline withdrew **for a** moment to the inner room. When **she re-** appeared Prince was startled.

" By Jove ! " he gasped. " Who 'd 'a' thought it ! The little witch ! Why, **my** sister " —

" Is an English girl," interrupted **Malemute** Kid, " with an English foot. This **girl comes** of a small-footed race. Moccasins **just broad-** ened her feet healthily, while she **did not** misshape them by running with the **dogs in** her childhood."

But this explanation failed utterly **to allay** Prince's admiration. Harrington's **commer-** cial instinct was touched, and as he **looked** upon the exquisitely turned foot and **ankle,** there ran through his mind the sordid **list,** — " one rifle, one blanket, twenty **bottles of** *hooch*."

Madeline was the wife of a king, a **king** whose yellow treasure could buy outright **a** score of fashion's puppets ; yet in **all her life** her feet had known no gear save **red-tanned** moosehide. At first she looked in awe at **the** tiny white satin slippers ; but she **quickly** understood the admiration which shone, **man-** like, in the eyes of the men. Her face **flushed**

with pride. For the moment she was drunken
with her woman's loveliness; then she murmured, with increased scorn, " And one rifle
broke ! "

So the training went on. Every day Malemute Kid led the girl out on long walks de-
voted to the correction of her carriage and
the shortening of her stride. There was little likelihood of her identity being discovered,
for Cal Galbraith and the rest of the Old-
Timers were like lost children among the
many strangers who had rushed into the land.
Besides, the frost of the North has a bitter
tongue, and the tender women of the South,
to shield their cheeks from its biting caresses,
were prone to the use of canvas masks. With
faces obscured and bodies lost in squirrel-skin
parkas, a mother and daughter, meeting on
trail, would pass as strangers.

The coaching progressed rapidly. At first
it had been slow, but later a sudden accelera-
tion had manifested itself. This began from
the moment Madeline tried on the white satin
slippers, and in so doing found herself. The
pride of her renegade father, apart from any
natural self-esteem she might possess, at that
instant received its birth. Hitherto, she had

deemed herself a woman of an alien breed, of
inferior stock, purchased by her lord's favor.
Her husband had seemed to her a god, who
had lifted her, through no essential virtues on
her part, to his own godlike level. But she
had never forgotten, even when young Cal
was born, that she was not of his people. As
he had been a god, so had his womankind
been goddesses. She might have contrasted
herself with them, but she had never com-
pared. It might have been that familiarity
bred contempt; however, be that as it may,
she had ultimately come to understand these
roving white men, and to weigh them. True,
her mind was dark to deliberate analysis, but
she yet possessed her woman's clarity of vision
in such matters. On the night of the slippers
she had measured the bold, open admiration
of her three man friends; and for the first
time comparison had suggested itself. It was
only a foot and an ankle, but — but comparison could not, in the nature of things, cease
at that point. She judged herself by their
standards till the divinity of her white sisters
was shattered. After all, they were only
women, and why should she not exalt herself
to their place? In doing these things she

learned where she lacked, and with the knowledge of her weakness came her strength.
And so mightily did she strive that her three
trainers often marveled late into the night
over the eternal mystery of woman.

In this way Thanksgiving night drew near.
At irregular intervals Bettles sent word down
from Stuart River regarding the welfare of
young Cal. The time of their return was
approaching. More than once a casual caller,
hearing dance-music and the rhythmic pulse
of feet, entered, only to find Harrington
scraping away and the other two beating time
or arguing noisily over a mooted step. Madeline was never in evidence, having precipi-
tately fled to the inner room.

On one of these nights Cal Galbraith
dropped in. Encouraging news had just
come down from Stuart River, and Madeline
had surpassed herself — not in walk alone,
and carriage and grace, but in womanly
roguishness. They had indulged in sharp re-
partee, and she had defended herself bril-
liantly ; and then, yielding to the intoxica-
tion of the moment, and of her own power,
she had bullied, and mastered, and wheedled,
and patronized them with most astonishing

success. And instinctively, involuntarily, they had bowed, not to her beauty, her wisdom, her wit, but to that indefinable something in woman to which man yields yet cannot name. The room was dizzy with sheer delight as she and Prince whirled through the last dance of the evening. Harrington was throwing in inconceivable flourishes, while Malemute Kid, utterly abandoned, had seized the broom and was executing mad gyrations on his own account.

At this instant the door shook with a heavy rap-rap, and their quick glances noted the lifting of the latch. But they had survived similar situations before. Harrington never broke a note. Madeline shot through the waiting door to the inner room. The broom went hurtling under the bunk, and by the time Cal Galbraith and Louis Savoy got their heads in, Malemute Kid and Prince were in each other's arms, wildly schottisching down the room.

As a rule, Indian women do not make a practice of fainting on provocation, but Madeline came as near to it as she ever had in her life. For an hour she crouched on the floor, listening to the heavy voices of the men

rumbling up and down in mimic thunder.
Like familiar chords of childhood melodies,
every intonation, every trick of her husband's
voice, swept in upon her, fluttering her heart
and weakening her knees till she lay half-
fainting against the door. It was well she
could neither see nor hear when he took his
departure.

"When do you expect to go back to Circle City?" Malemute Kid asked simply.

"Have n't thought much about it," he replied. "Don't think till after the ice breaks."

"And Madeline?"

He flushed at the question, and there was
a quick droop to his eyes. Malemute Kid
could have despised him for that, had he
known men less. As it was, his gorge rose
against the wives and daughters who had
come into the land, and not satisfied with
usurping the place of the native women, had
put unclean thoughts in the heads of the
men and made them ashamed.

"I guess she 's all right," the Circle City
king answered hastily, and in an apologetic
manner. "Tom Dixon 's got charge of my
interests, you know, and he sees to it that
she has everything she wants."

Malemute Kid laid hand upon his arm, and
hushed him suddenly. They had stepped without. Overhead, the aurora, a gorgeous wanton,
flaunted miracles of color; beneath lay the
sleeping town. Far below, a solitary dog gave
tongue. The king again began to speak, but
the Kid pressed his hand for silence. The
sound multiplied. Dog after dog took up the
strain till the full-throated chorus swayed the
night. To him who hears for the first time
this weird song, is told the first and greatest
secret of the Northland; to him who has
heard it often, it is the solemn knell of lost
endeavor. It is the plaint of tortured souls,
for in it is invested the heritage of the North,
the suffering of countless generations — the
warning and the requiem to the world s es-
trays.

Cal Galbraith shivered slightly as it died
away in half-caught sobs. The Kid read his
thoughts openly, and wandered back with him
through all the weary days of famine and disease; and with him was also the patient
Madeline, sharing his pains and perils, never
doubting, never complaining. His mind's re-
tina vibrated to a score of pictures, stern,
clear-cut, and the hand of the Past drew back

with heavy fingers on his heart. It was the
psychological moment. Malemute Kid was
half tempted to play his reserve card and win
the game; but the lesson was too mild as yet,
and he let it pass. The next instant they had
gripped hands, and the king's beaded moccasins were drawing protests from the outraged
snow as he crunched down the hill.

Madeline in collapse was another woman to
the mischievous creature of an hour before,
whose laughter had been so infectious and
whose heightened color and flashing eyes had
made her teachers for the while forget. Weak
and nerveless, she sat in the chair just as
she had been dropped there by Prince and
Harrington. Malemute Kid frowned. This
would never do. When the time of meeting
her husband came to hand, she must carry
things off with high-handed imperiousness.
It was very necessary she should do it after
the manner of white women, else the victory
would be no victory at all. So he talked to
her, sternly, without mincing of words, and
initiated her into the weaknesses of his own
sex, till she came to understand what simple-
tons men were after all, and why the word
of their women was law.

A few days before Thanksgiving night,
Malemute Kid made another call on Mrs.
Eppingwell. She promptly overhauled her
feminine fripperies, paid a protracted visit to
the dry-goods department of the P. C. Company, and returned with the Kid to make
Madeline's acquaintance. After that came a
period such as the cabin had never seen before, and what with cutting, and fitting, and
basting, and stitching, and numerous other
wonderful and unknowable things, the male
conspirators were more often banished the
premises than not. At such times the Opera
House opened its double storm-doors to them.
So often did they put their heads together,
and so deeply did they drink to curious toasts,
that the loungers scented unknown creeks of
incalculable richness, and it is known that
several *che-cha-quas* and at least one Old-
Timer kept their stampeding packs stored
behind the bar, ready to hit the trail at a
moment's notice.

Mrs. Eppingwell was a woman of capacity ;
so, when she turned Madeline over to her
trainers on Thanksgiving night she was so
transformed that they were almost afraid of her.
Prince wrapped a Hudson Bay blanket about

her with a mock reverence more real than
feigned, while Malemute Kid, whose arm she
had taken, found it a severe trial to resume
his wonted mentorship. Harrington, with the
list of purchase still running through his
head, dragged along in the rear, nor opened
his mouth once all the way down into the
town. When they came to the back door of
the Opera House they took the blanket from
Madeline's shoulders and spread it on the
snow. Slipping out of Prince's moccasins, she
stepped upon it in new satin slippers. The
masquerade was at its height. She hesitated,
but they jerked open the door and shoved
her in. Then they ran around to come in by
the front entrance.

III

" Where is Freda ? " the Old-Timers questioned, while the *che-cha-quas* were equally
energetic in asking who Freda was. The ball-
room buzzed with her name. It was on
everybody's lips. Grizzled " sour-dough boys,"
day-laborers at the mines but proud of their
degree, either patronized the spruce-looking
tenderfeet and lied eloquently, — the " sour-
dough boys " being specially created to toy

with truth, — or gave them savage looks of
indignation because of their ignorance. Perhaps forty kings of the Upper and Lower
Countries were on the floor, each deeming
himself hot on the trail and sturdily backing
his judgment with the yellow dust of the
realm. An assistant was sent to the man at
the scales, upon whom had fallen the burden
of weighing up the sacks, while several of
the gamblers, with the rules of chance at their
finger-ends, made up alluring books on the
field and favorites.

Which was Freda ? Time and again the
Greek dancer was thought to have been discovered, but each discovery brought panic to
the betting ring and a frantic registering of
new wagers by those who wished to hedge.
Malemute Kid took an interest in the hunt,
his advent being hailed uproariously by the
revelers, who knew him to a man. The Kid
had a good eye for the trick of a step, and
ear for the lilt of a voice, and his private choice
was a marvelous creature who scintillated as
the " Aurora Borealis."   But the Greek
dancer was too subtle for even his penetration.
The majority of the gold-hunters seemed to
have centred their verdict on the " Russian

Princess," who was the most graceful in the room, and hence could be no other than Freda Moloof.

During a quadrille a roar of satisfaction went up. She was discovered. At previous balls, in the figure " all hands round," Freda had displayed an inimitable step and variation peculiarly her own. As the figure was called, the " Russian Princess " gave the unique rhythm to limb and body. A chorus of I-told-you-so's shook the squared roof-beams, when lo ! it was noticed that the " Aurora Borealis " and another mask, the " Spirit of the Pole," were performing the same trick equally well. And when two twin " Sun-Dogs " and a " Frost Queen " followed suit, a second assistant was dispatched to the aid of the man at the scales.

Bettles came off trail in the midst of the excitement, descending upon them in a hurricane of frost. His rimed brows turned to cataracts as he whirled about ; his mustache, still frozen, seemed gemmed with diamonds and turned the light in vari-colored rays ; while the flying feet slipped on the chunks of ice which rattled from his moccasins and German socks. A Northland dance is quite an informal affair, the men of the creeks and trails having lost whatever fastidiousness they may have at one time possessed; and only in the high official circles are conventions at all observed. Here, caste carried no significance. Millionaires and paupers, dog-drivers and mounted policemen, joined hands with "ladies in the centre," and swept around the circle performing most remarkable capers. Primitive in their pleasures, boisterous and rough, they displayed no rudeness, but rather a crude chivalry as genuine as the most polished courtesy.

In his quest for the Greek dancer, Cal Galbraith managed to get into the same set with the "Russian Princess," toward whom popular suspicion had turned. But by the time he had guided her through one dance, he was willing not only to stake his millions that she was not Freda, but that he had had his arm about her waist before. When or where he could not tell, but the puzzling sense of familiarity so wrought upon him that he turned his attention to the discovery of her identity. Malemute Kid might have aided him instead of occasionally taking the "Princess" for a few turns and talking earnestly to her in low tones. But it was Jack Harrington who

paid the " Russian Princess " the most assidu-
ous court. Once he drew Cal Galbraith aside
and hazarded wild guesses as to who she was,
and explained to him that he was going in
to win. This rankled the Circle City king,
for man is not by nature monogamic, and he
forgot both Madeline and Freda in the new
quest.

It was soon noised about that the " Russian
Princess " was not Freda Moloof. Interest
deepened. Here was a fresh enigma. They
knew Freda though they could not find her,
but here was somebody they had found and
did not know. Even the women could not
place her, and they knew every good dancer
in the camp. Many took her for one of the
official clique, indulging in a silly escapade.
Not a few asserted she would disappear before
the unmasking. Others were equally positive
that she was the woman reporter of the Kan-
sas City " Star," come to write them up at
ninety dollars per column. And the men at
the scales worked busily.

At one o'clock every couple took to the
floor. The unmasking began amid laughter
and delight, like that of care-free children.
There was no end of oh's and ah's as mask

after mask was lifted. The scintillating
" Aurora Borealis " became the brawny ne-
gress whose income from washing the community's clothes ran at about five hundred a
month. The twin " Sun-Dogs " discovered
mustaches on their upper lips, and were recognized as brother fraction-kings of Eldorado.
In one of the most prominent sets, and
the slowest in uncovering, was Cal Galbraith
with the " Spirit of the Pole." Opposite him
was Jack Harrington and the " Russian Princess." The rest had discovered themselves,
yet the Greek dancer was still missing. All
eyes were upon the group. Cal Galbraith,
in response to their cries, lifted his partner's
mask. Freda's wonderful face and brilliant
eyes flashed out upon them. A roar went
up, to be hushed suddenly in the new and
absorbing mystery of the "Russian Princess."
Her face was still hidden, and Jack Harrington was struggling with her. The dancers
tittered on the tiptoes of expectancy. He
crushed her dainty costume roughly, and
then — and then the revelers exploded. The
joke was on them. They had danced all
night with a tabooed native woman.

But those that knew, and they were many,

ceased abruptly, and a hush fell upon the room. Cal Galbraith crossed over with great strides, angrily, and spoke to Madeline in polyglot Chinook. But she retained her composure, apparently oblivious to the fact that she was the cynosure of all eyes, and answered him in English. She showed neither fright nor anger, and Malemute Kid chuckled at her well-bred equanimity. The king felt baffled, defeated; his common Siwash wife had passed beyond him.

"Come!" he said finally. "Come on home."

"I beg pardon," she replied; "I have agreed to go to supper with Mr. Harrington. Besides, there's no end of dances promised."

Harrington extended his arm to lead her away. He evinced not the slightest disinclination toward showing his back, but Malemute Kid had by this time edged in closer. The Circle City king was stunned. Twice his hand dropped to his belt, and twice the Kid gathered himself to spring; but the retreating couple passed safely through the supper-room door, where canned oysters were spread at five dollars the plate. The crowd sighed audibly, broke up into couples, and followed them. Freda pouted and went in with Cal Galbraith; but she had a good heart and a sure tongue, and she spoiled his oysters for him. What she said is of no importance, but his face went red and white at intervals, and he swore repeatedly and savagely at himself.

The supper-room was filled with a pandemonium of voices, which ceased suddenly as Cal Galbraith stepped over to his wife's table. Since the unmasking considerable weights of dust had been placed as to the outcome. Everybody watched with breathless interest. Harrington's blue eyes were steady, but under the over-hanging tablecloth a Smith & Wesson balanced on his knee. Madeline looked up, casually, with little interest.

"May — may I have the next round dance with you?" the king stuttered.

The wife of the king glanced at her card and inclined her head.

AN ODYSSEY OF THE NORTH

I

THE sleds were singing their eternal lament to the creaking of the harnesses and the tinkling bells of the leaders; but the men and dogs were tired and made no sound. The trail was heavy with new-fallen snow, and they had come far, and the runners, burdened with flint-like quarters of frozen moose, clung tenaciously to the unpacked surface and held back with a stubbornness almost human. Darkness was coming on, but there was no camp to pitch that night. The snow fell gently through the pulseless air, not in flakes, but in tiny frost crystals of delicate design. It was very warm, — barely ten below zero, — and the men did not mind. Meyers and Bettles had raised their ear-flaps, while Malemute Kid had even taken off his mittens.

The dogs had been fagged out early in the afternoon, but they now began to show new

vigor. Among the more astute there was a
certain restlessness, — an impatience at the
restraint of the traces, an indecisive quick-
ness of movement, a sniffing of snouts and
pricking of ears. These became incensed at
their more phlegmatic brothers, urging them
on with numerous sly nips on their hinder-
quarters. Those, thus chidden, also con-
tracted and helped spread the contagion.
At last, the leader of the foremost sled ut-
tered a sharp whine of satisfaction, crouching
lower in the snow and throwing himself
against the collar. The rest followed suit.
There was an ingathering of back-bands, a
tightening of traces ; the sleds leaped forward, and the men clung to the gee-poles,
violently accelerating the uplift of their feet
that they might escape going under the runners. The weariness of the day fell from
them, and they whooped encouragement to
the dogs. The animals responded with joyous yelps. They were swinging through the
gathering darkness at a rattling gallop.

" Gee ! Gee ! " the men cried, each in turn,
as their sleds abruptly left the main-trail,
heeling over on single runners like luggers
on the wind.

Then came a hundred yards' dash to the lighted parchment window, which told its own story of the home cabin, the roaring Yukon stove, and the steaming pots of tea. But the home cabin had been invaded. Three-score huskies chorused defiance, and as many furry forms precipitated themselves upon the dogs which drew the first sled. The door was flung open, and a man, clad in the scarlet tunic of the Northwest Police, waded knee-deep among the furious brutes, calmly and impartially dispensing soothing justice with the butt end of a dog-whip. After that, the men shook hands ; and in this wise was Malemute Kid welcomed to his own cabin by a stranger.

Stanley Prince, who should have welcomed him, and who was responsible for the Yukon stove and hot tea aforementioned, was busy with his guests. There were a dozen or so of them, as nondescript a crowd as ever served the Queen in the enforcement of her laws or the delivery of her mails. They were of many breeds, but their common life had formed of them a certain type, — a lean and wiry type, with trail-hardened muscles, and sun-browned faces, and untroubled souls which gazed frankly forth, clear-eyed and steady. They drove the dogs of the Queen, wrought fear in the hearts of her enemies, ate of her meagre fare, and were happy. They had seen life, and done deeds, and lived romances ; but they did not know it.

And they were very much at home. Two of them were sprawled upon Malemute Kid's bunk, singing chansons which their French forbears sang in the days when first they entered the Northwest-land and mated with its Indian women. Bettles' bunk had suffered a similar invasion, and three or four lusty *voyageurs* worked their toes among its blankets as they listened to the tale of one who had served on the boat brigade with Wolseley when he fought his way to Khartoum. And when he tired, a cowboy told of courts and kings and lords and ladies he had seen when Buffalo Bill toured the capitals of Europe. In a corner, two halfbreeds, ancient comrades in a lost campaign, mended harnesses and talked of the days when the Northwest flamed with insurrection and Louis Reil was king.

Rough jests and rougher jokes went up and down, and great hazards by trail and river were spoken of in the light of commonplaces, only to be recalled by virtue of some grain of humor or ludicrous happening. Prince was led away by these uncrowned heroes who had seen history made, who regarded the great and the romantic as but the ordinary and the incidental in the routine of life. He passed his precious tobacco among them with lavish disregard, and rusty chains of reminiscence were loosened, and forgotten odysseys resurrected for his especial benefit.

When conversation dropped and the travelers filled the last pipes and unlashed their tight-rolled sleeping-furs, Prince fell back upon his comrade for further information.

"Well, you know what the cowboy is," Malemute Kid answered, beginning to unlace his moccasins; "and it's not hard to guess the British blood in his bed-partner. As for the rest, they're all children of the *coureurs du bois*, mingled with God knows how many other bloods. The two turning in by the door are the regulation 'breeds' or *bois brulés*. That lad with the worsted breech scarf — notice his eyebrows and the turn of his jaw — shows a Scotchman wept in his mother's smoky tepee. And that handsome-looking fellow putting the capote under his head is a French half-breed, — you heard him talking; he does n't like the two Indians turning in next to him. You see, when the ' breeds ' rose under Reil the full-bloods kept the peace, and they've not lost much love for one another since."

" But I say, what 's that glum-looking fellow by the stove? I 'll swear he can't talk English. He has n't opened his mouth all night."

" You 're wrong. He knows English well enough. Did you follow his eyes when he listened ? I did. But he 's neither kith nor kin to the others. When they talked their own patois you could see he did n't understand. I 've been wondering myself what he is. Let's find out."

" Fire a couple of sticks into the stove ! " Malemute Kid commanded, raising his voice and looking squarely at the man in question.

He obeyed at once.

" Had discipline knocked into him somewhere," Prince commented in a low tone.

Malemute Kid nodded, took off his socks, and picked his way among the recumbent men to the stove. There he hung his damp footgear among a score or so of mates.

"When do you expect to get to Dawson?" he asked tentatively.

The man studied him a moment before replying. "They say seventy-five mile. So? Maybe two days."

The very slightest accent was perceptible, while there was no awkward hesitancy or groping for words.

"Been in the country before?"

"No."

"Northwest Territory?"

"Yes."

"Born there?"

"No."

"Well, where the devil were you born? You're none of these." Malemute Kid swept his hand over the dog-drivers, even including the two policemen who had turned into Prince's bunk. "Where did you come from? I've seen faces like yours before, though I can't remember just where."

"I know you," he irrelevantly replied, at once turning the drift of Malemute Kid's questions.

"Where? Ever see me?"

"No; your partner, him priest, Pastilik, long time ago. Him ask me if I see you,

Malemute Kid. Him give me grub. I no stop long. You hear him speak 'bout me?"

"Oh! you're the fellow that traded the otter skins for the dogs?"

The man nodded, knocked out his pipe, and signified his disinclination for conversation by rolling up in his furs. Malemute Kid blew out the slush-lamp and crawled under the blankets with Prince.

"Well, what is he?"

"Don't know — turned me off, somehow, and then shut up like a clam. But he's a fellow to whet your curiosity. I've heard of him. All the Coast wondered about him eight years ago. Sort of mysterious, you know. He came down out of the North, in the dead of winter, many a thousand miles from here, skirting Bering Sea and traveling as though the devil were after him. No one ever learned where he came from, but he must have come far. He was badly travel-worn when he got food from the Swedish missionary on Golovin Bay and asked the way south. We heard of this afterward. Then he abandoned the shore-line, heading right across Norton Sound. Terrible weather, snowstorms and high winds, but he pulled through where a thousand other men would have died, missing St. Michael's and making the land at Pastilik. He'd lost all but two dogs, and was nearly gone with starvation.

" He was so anxious to go on that Father Roubeau fitted him out with grub; but he could n't let him have any dogs, for he was only waiting my arrival to go on a trip himself. Mr. Ulysses knew too much to start on without animals, and fretted around for several days. He had on his sled a bunch of beautifully cured otter skins, sea-otters, you know, worth their weight in gold. There was also at Pastilik an old Shylock of a Russian trader, who had dogs to kill. Well, they did n't dicker very long, but when the Strange One headed south again, it was in the rear of a spanking dog-team. Mr. Shylock, by the way, had the otter skins. I saw them, and they were magnificent. We figured it up and found the dogs brought him at least five hundred apiece. And it was n't as if the Strange One did n't know the value of sea-otter; he was an Indian of some sort, and what little he talked showed he'd been among white men.

" After the ice passed out of the Sea, word

came up from Nunivak Island that he'd gone in there for grub. Then he dropped from sight, and this is the first heard of him in eight years. Now where did he come from? and what was he doing there? and why did he come from there? He's Indian, he's been nobody knows where, and he's had discipline, which is unusual for an Indian. Another mystery of the North for you to solve, Prince."

"Thanks, awfully; but I've got too many on hand as it is," he replied.

Malemute Kid was already breathing heavily; but the young mining engineer gazed straight up through the thick darkness, waiting for the strange orgasm which stirred his blood to die away. And when he did sleep, his brain worked on, and for the nonce he, too, wandered through the white unknown, struggled with the dogs on endless trails, and saw men live, and toil, and die like men.

The next morning, hours before daylight, the dog-drivers and policemen pulled out for Dawson. But the powers that saw to her Majesty's interests, and ruled the destinies of her lesser creatures, gave the mailmen little rest; for a week later they appeared at Stuart River, heavily burdened with letters for Salt Water. However, their dogs had been replaced by fresh ones; but then, they were dogs.

The men had expected some sort of a lay-over in which to rest up; besides, this Klondike was a new section of the Northland, and they had wished to see a little something of the Golden City where dust flowed like water, and dance halls rang with never ending revelry. But they dried their socks and smoked their evening pipes with much the same gusto as on their former visit, though one or two bold spirits speculated on desertion and the possibility of crossing the unexplored Rockies to the east, and thence, by the Mackenzie Valley, of gaining their old stamping-grounds in the Chippewyan Country. Two or three even decided to return to their homes by that route when their terms of service had expired, and they began to lay plans forthwith, looking forward to the hazardous undertaking in much the same way a city-bred man would to a day's holiday in the woods.

He of the Otter Skins seemed very restless,

though he took little interest in the discussion, and at last he drew Malemute Kid to one side and talked for some time in low tones. Prince cast curious eyes in their direction, and the mystery deepened when they put on caps and mittens, and went outside. When they returned, Malemute Kid placed his gold-scales on the table, weighed out the matter of sixty ounces, and transferred them to the Strange One's sack. Then the chief of the dog-drivers joined the conclave, and certain business was transacted with him. The next day the gang went on up river, but He of the Otter Skins took several pounds of grub and turned his steps back toward Dawson.

"Did n't know what to make of it," said Malemute Kid in response to Prince's queries; "but the poor beggar wanted to be quit of the service for some reason or other — at least it seemed a most important one to him, though he would n't let on what. You see, it 's just like the army; he signed for two years, and the only way to get free was to buy himself out. He could n't desert and then stay here, and he was just wild to remain in the country. Made up his mind

when he got to Dawson, he said; but no
one knew him, had n't a cent, and I was the
only one he 'd spoken two words with.   So
he talked it over with the Lieutenant-Gov-
ernor, and made arrangements in case he
could get the money from me — loan, you
know.   Said he 'd pay back in the year, and
if I wanted, would put me onto something
rich.   Never 'd seen it, but knew it was rich.

"And talk! why, when he got me outside
he was ready to weep.   Begged and pleaded;
got down in the snow to me till I hauled
him out of it.   Palavered around like a crazy
man.   Swore he 's worked to this very end
for years and years, and could n't bear to be
disappointed now.   Asked him what end,
but he would n't say.   Said they might keep
him on the other half of the trail and he
would n't get to Dawson in two years, and
then it would be too late.   Never saw a man
take on so in my life.   And when I said I 'd
let him have it, had to yank him out of the
snow again.   Told him to consider it in the
light of a grub-stake.   Think he 'd have it?
No, sir!   Swore he 'd give me all he found,
make me rich beyond the dreams of avarice,
and all such stuff.   Now a man who puts his

life and time against a grub-stake ordinarily finds it hard enough to turn over half of what he finds. Something behind all this, Prince; just you make a note of it. We'll hear of him if he stays in the country"—

"And if he does n't?"

"Then my good nature gets a shock, and I'm sixty some odd ounces out."

The cold weather had come on with the long nights, and the sun had begun to play his ancient game of peekaboo along the southern snow-line ere aught was heard of Malemute Kid's grub-stake. And then, one bleak morning in early January, a heavily laden dog-train pulled into his cabin below Stuart River. He of the Otter Skins was there, and with him walked a man such as the gods have almost forgotten how to fashion. Men never talked of luck and pluck and five-hundred-dollar dirt without bringing in the name of Axel Gunderson; nor could tales of nerve or strength or daring pass up and down the camp-fire without the summoning of his presence. And when the conversation flagged, it blazed anew at mention of the woman who shared his fortunes.

As has been noted, in the making of Axel Gunderson the gods had remembered their old-time cunning, and cast him after the manner of men who were born when the world was young. Full seven feet he towered in his picturesque costume which marked a king of Eldorado. His chest, neck, and limbs were those of a giant. To bear his three hundred pounds of bone and muscle, his snowshoes were greater by a generous yard than those of other men. Rough-hewn, with rugged brow and massive jaw and unflinching eyes of palest blue, his face told the tale of one who knew but the law of might. Of the yellow of ripe corn silk, his frost-incrusted hair swept like day across the night, and fell far down his coat of bearskin. A vague tradition of the sea seemed to cling about him, as he swung down the narrow trail in advance of the dogs; and he brought the butt of his dog-whip against Malemute Kid's door as a Norse sea rover, on southern foray, might thunder for admittance at the castle gate.

Prince bared his womanly arms and kneaded sour-dough bread, casting, as he did so, many a glance at the three guests,

— three guests the like of which might never come under a man's roof in a lifetime. The Strange One, whom Malemute Kid had surnamed Ulysses, still fascinated him; but his interest chiefly gravitated between Axel Gunderson and Axel Gunderson's wife. She felt the day's journey, for she had softened in comfortable cabins during the many days since her husband mastered the wealth of frozen pay-streaks, and she was tired. She rested against his great breast like a slender flower against a wall, replying lazily to Malemute Kid's good-natured banter, and stirring Prince's blood strangely with an occasional sweep of her deep, dark eyes. For Prince was a man, and healthy, and had seen few women in many months. And she was older than he, and an Indian besides. But she was different from all native wives he had met: she had traveled, — had been in his country among others, he gathered from the conversation; and she knew most of the things the women of his own race knew, and much more that it was not in the nature of things for them to know. She could make a meal of sun-dried fish or a bed in the snow; yet she teased them with tantalizing details of many-course dinners, and caused strange internal dissensions to arise at the mention of various quondam dishes which they had well-nigh forgotten. She knew the ways of the moose, the bear, and the little blue fox, and of the wild amphibians of the Northern seas; she was skilled in the lore of the woods and the streams, and the tale writ by man and bird and beast upon the delicate snow crust was to her an open book; yet Prince caught the appreciative twinkle in her eye as she read the Rules of the Camp. These rules had been fathered by the Unquenchable Bettles at a time when his blood ran high, and were remarkable for the terse simplicity of their humor. Prince always turned them to the wall before the arrival of ladies; but who could suspect that this native wife — Well, it was too late now.

This, then, was the wife of Axel Gunderson, a woman whose name and fame had traveled with her husband's, hand in hand, through all the Northland. At table, Malemute Kid baited her with the assurance of an old friend, and Prince shook off the shyness of first acquaintance and joined in. But she held her own in the unequal contest, while her husband, slower in wit, ventured naught but applause. And he was very proud of her; his every look and action revealed the magnitude of the place she occupied in his life. He of the Otter Skins ate in silence, forgotten in the merry battle; and long ere the others were done he pushed back from the table and went out among the dogs. Yet all too soon his fellow travelers drew on their mittens and *parkas*, and followed him.

There had been no snow for many days, and the sleds slipped along the hard-packed Yukon trail as easily as if it had been glare ice. Ulysses led the first sled; with the second came Prince and Axel Gunderson's wife; while Malemute Kid and the yellow-haired giant brought up the third.

"It's only a 'hunch,' Kid," he said; "but I think it's straight. He's never been there, but he tells a good story, and shows a map I heard of when I was in the Kootenay country, years ago. I'd like to have you go along; but he's a strange one, and swore point-blank to throw it up if any one was brought in. But when I come back you'll get first tip, and I'll stake you next to me, and give you a half share in the town site besides.

"No! no!" he cried, as the other strove to interrupt. "I'm running this, and before I'm done it'll need two heads. If it's all right, why it'll be a second Cripple Creek, man; do you hear? — a second Cripple Creek! It's quartz, you know, not placer; and if we work it right we'll corral the whole thing, — millions upon millions. I've heard of the place before, and so have you. We'll build a town — thousands of workmen — good waterways — steamship lines — big carrying trade — light-draught steamers for head-reaches — survey a railroad, perhaps — sawmills — electric-light plant — do our own banking — commercial company — syndicate — Say! just you hold your hush till I get back!"

The sleds came to a halt where the trail crossed the mouth of Stuart River. An unbroken sea of frost, its wide expanse stretched away into the unknown east. The snowshoes were withdrawn from the lashings of the sleds. Axel Gunderson shook hands and stepped to the fore, his great webbed shoes sinking a fair half yard into the feathery surface and packing the snow so the dogs should not wallow. His wife fell in behind the last

sled, betraying long practice in the art of
handling the awkward footgear. The stillness was broken with cheery farewells; the
dogs whined; and He of the Otter Skins
talked with his whip to a recalcitrant wheeler.

An hour later, the train had taken on the
likeness of a black pencil crawling in a long,
straight line across a mighty sheet of fools-
cap.

II

One night, many weeks later, Malemute
Kid and Prince fell to solving chess problems
from the torn page of an ancient magazine.
The Kid had just returned from his Bonanza
properties, and was resting up preparatory to
a long moose hunt. Prince too had been on
creek and trail nearly all winter, and had
grown hungry for a blissful week of cabin
life.

" Interpose the black knight, and force the
king. No, that won't do. See, the next
move " —

" Why advance the pawn two squares?
Bound to take it in transit, and with the
bishop out of the way " —

" But hold on! That leaves a hole,
and " —

"No; it's protected.   Go ahead!   You'll see it works."

It was very interesting.   Somebody knocked at the door a second time before Malemute Kid said, "Come in."   The door swung open. Something staggered in.   Prince caught one square look, and sprang to his feet.   The horror in his eyes caused Malemute Kid to whirl about; and he too was startled, though he had seen bad things before.   The thing tottered blindly toward them.   Prince edged away till he reached the nail from which hung his Smith & Wesson.

"My God! what is it?" he whispered to Malemute Kid.

"Don't know.   Looks like a case of freezing and no grub," replied the Kid, sliding away in the opposite direction.   "Watch out!   It may be mad," he warned, coming back from closing the door.

The thing advanced to the table.   The bright flame of the slush-lamp caught its eye. It was amused, and gave voice to eldritch cackles which betokened mirth.   Then, suddenly, he — for it was a man — swayed back, with a hitch to his skin trousers, and began to sing a chanty, such as men lift when they

swing around the capstan circle and the sea
snorts in their ears : —

> " Yan-kee ship come down de ri-ib-er,
>   Pull ! my bully boys !   Pull !
> D'yeh want — to know de captain ru-uns her ?
>   Pull ! my bully boys !   Pull !
> Jon-a-than Jones ob South Caho-li-in-a,
>   Pull ! my bully " —

He broke off abruptly, tottered with a wolfish snarl to the meat-shelf, and before they
could intercept was tearing with his teeth at a
chunk of raw bacon. The struggle was fierce
between him and Malemute Kid ; but his mad
strength left him as suddenly as it had come,
and he weakly surrendered the spoil. Between
them they got him upon a stool, where he
sprawled with half his body across the table.
A small dose of whiskey strengthened him,
so that he could dip a spoon into the sugar
caddy which Malemute Kid placed before him.
After his appetite had been somewhat cloyed,
Prince, shuddering as he did so, passed him a
mug of weak beef tea.

The creature's eyes were alight with a som-
bre frenzy, which blazed and waned with
every mouthful. There was very little skin
to the face. The face, for that matter, sunken
and emaciated, bore very little likeness to

human countenance. Frost after frost had bitten deeply, each depositing its stratum of scab upon the half-healed scar that went before. This dry, hard surface was of a bloody-black color, serrated by grievous cracks wherein the raw red flesh peeped forth. His skin garments were dirty and in tatters, and the fur of one side was singed and burned away, showing where he had lain upon his fire.

Malemute Kid pointed to where the sun-tanned hide had been cut away, strip by strip, — the grim signature of famine.

" Who — are — you ? " slowly and distinctly enunciated the Kid.

The man paid no heed.

" Where do you come from ? "

" Yan-kee ship come down de ri-ib-er," was the quavering response.

" Don't doubt the beggar came down the river," the Kid said, shaking him in an endeavor to start a more lucid flow of talk.

But the man shrieked at the contact, clapping a hand to his side in evident pain. He rose slowly to his feet, half leaning on the table.

" She laughed at me — so — with the hate in her eye ; and she — would — not — come."

His voice died away, and he was sinking back when Malemute Kid gripped him by the wrist, and shouted, " Who? Who would not come ? "

" She, Unga. She laughed, and struck at me, so, and so. And then " —

" Yes ? "

" And then " —

" And then what ? "

" And then he lay very still, in the snow, a long time. He is — still in — the — snow."

The two men looked at each other helplessly.

" Who is in the snow ? "

" She, Unga. She looked at me with the hate in her eye, and then " —

" Yes, yes."

" And then she took the knife, so; and once, twice — she was weak. I traveled very slow. And there is much gold in that place, very much gold."

" Where is Unga? " For all Malemute Kid knew, she might be dying a mile away. He shook the man savagely, repeating again and again, " Where is Unga ? Who is Unga ? "

" She — is — in — the — snow."

" Go on ! " The Kid was pressing his wrist cruelly.

" So — I — would — be — in — the snow — but — I — had — a — debt — to — pay. It — was — heavy — I — had — a — debt — to — pay — a — debt — to — pay — I — had " — The faltering monosyllables ceased, as he fumbled in his pouch and drew forth a buckskin sack. " A — debt — to — pay — five — pounds — of — gold — grub — stake — Mal — e — mute — Kid — I " — The exhausted head dropped upon the table ; nor could Malemute Kid rouse it again.

" It 's 'Ulysses," he said quietly, tossing the bag of dust on the table. " Guess it 's all day with Axel Gunderson and the woman. Come on, let 's get him between the blankets. He 's Indian ; he 'll pull through, and tell a tale besides."

As they cut his garments from him, near his right breast could be seen two unhealed, hard-lipped knife thrusts.

III

" I will talk of the things which were, in my own way ; but you will understand. I will begin at the beginning, and tell of myself and the woman, and, after that, of the man."

He of the Otter Skins drew over to the
stove as do men who have been deprived
of fire and are afraid the Promethean gift
may vanish at any moment. Malemute Kid
pricked up the slush-lamp, and placed it so
its light might fall upon the face of the nar-
rator.   Prince slid his body over the edge of
the bunk and joined them.

"I am Naass, a chief, and the son of a
chief, born between a sunset and a rising, on
the dark seas, in my father's oomiak.   All
of a night the men toiled at the paddles, and
the women cast out the waves which threw in
upon us, and we fought with the storm. The
salt spray froze upon my mother's breast till
her breath passed with the passing of the
tide.   But I, — I raised my voice with the
wind and the storm, and lived.

"We dwelt in Akatan" —

"Where?" asked Malemute Kid.

"Akatan, which is in the Aleutians; Akatan, beyond Chignik, beyond Kardalak, beyond Unimak.   As I say, we dwelt in Akatan, which lies in the midst of the sea on the
edge of the world.   We farmed the salt seas
for the fish, the seal, and the otter; and our
homes shouldered about one another on the

rocky strip between the rim of the forest and the yellow beach where our kayaks lay. We were not many, and the world was very small. There were strange lands to the east, — islands like Akatan; so we thought all the world was islands, and did not mind.

"I was different from my people. In the sands of the beach were the crooked timbers and wave-warped planks of a boat such as my people never built; and I remember on the point of the island which overlooked the ocean three ways there stood a pine tree which never grew there, smooth and straight and tall. It is said the two men came to that spot, turn about, through many days, and watched with the passing of the light. These two men came from out of the sea in the boat which lay in pieces on the beach. And they were white like you, and weak as the little children when the seal have gone away and the hunters come home empty. I know of these things from the old men and the old women, who got them from their fathers and mothers before them. These strange white men did not take kindly to our ways at first, but they grew strong, what of the fish and the oil, and fierce. And they built them each his own house, and took the pick of our women, and in time children came. Thus he was born who was to become the father of my father's father.

"As I said, I was different from my people, for I carried the strong, strange blood of this white man who came out of the sea. It is said we had other laws in the days before these men ; but they were fierce and quarrelsome, and fought with our men till there were no more left who dared to fight. Then they made themselves chiefs, and took away our old laws and gave us new ones, insomuch that the man was the son of his father, and not his mother, as our way had been. They also ruled that the son, firstborn, should have all things which were his father's before him, and that the brothers and sisters should shift for themselves. And they gave us other laws. They showed us new ways in the catching of fish and the killing of bear which were thick in the woods; and they taught us to lay by bigger stores for the time of famine. And these things were good.

"But when they had become chiefs, and there were no more men to face their anger, they fought, these strange white men, each

with the other. And the one whose blood I
carry drove his seal spear the length of an
arm through the other's body. Their children took up the fight, and their children's
children ; and there was great hatred between
them, and black doings, even to my time, so
that in each family but one lived to pass down
the blood of them that went before. Of my
blood I was alone ; of the other man's there
was but a girl, Unga, who lived with her
mother. Her father and my father did not
come back from the fishing one night ; but
afterward they washed up to the beach on
the big tides, and they held very close to
each other.

"The people wondered, because of the
hatred between the houses, and the old men
shook their heads and said the fight would
go on when children were born to her and
children to me. They told me this as a boy,
till I came to believe, and to look upon Unga
as a foe, who was to be the mother of children
which were to fight with mine. I thought of
these things day by day, and when I grew to a
stripling I came to ask why this should be so.
And they answered, ' We do not know, but
that in such way your fathers did.' And I

marveled that those which were to come should
fight the battles of those that were gone, and
in it I could see no right. But the people
said it must be, and I was only a stripling.

"And they said I must hurry, that my
blood might be the older and grow strong before hers. This was easy, for I was head
man, and the people looked up to me because
of the deeds and the laws of my fathers, and
the wealth which was mine. Any maiden
would come to me, but I found none to my
liking. And the old men and the mothers
of maidens told me to hurry, for even then
were the hunters bidding high to the mother
of Unga; and should her children grow
strong before mine, mine would surely die.

"Nor did I find a maiden till one night
coming back from the fishing. The sunlight
was lying, so, low and full in the eyes, the
wind free, and the kayaks racing with the
white seas. Of a sudden the kayak of Unga
came driving past me, and she looked upon
me, so, with her black hair flying like a cloud
of night and the spray wet on her cheek.
As I say, the sunlight was full in the eyes,
and I was a stripling; but somehow it was
all clear, and I knew it to be the call of kind

to kind. As she whipped ahead she looked
back within the space of two strokes, —
looked as only the woman Unga could look,
— and again I knew it as the call of kind.
The people shouted as we ripped past the
lazy oomiaks and left them far behind. But
she was quick at the paddle, and my heart
was like the belly of a sail, and I did not
gain. The wind freshened, the sea whitened,
and, leaping like the seals on the windward
breech, we roared down the golden pathway
of the sun."

Naass was crouched half out of his stool,
in the attitude of one driving a paddle, as he
ran the race anew. Somewhere across the
stove he beheld the tossing kayak and the
flying hair of Unga. The voice of the wind
was in his ears, and its salt beat fresh upon
his nostrils.

"But she made the shore, and ran up the
sand, laughing, to the house of her mother.
And a great thought came to me that night,
— a thought worthy of him that was chief
over all the people of Akatan. So, when the
moon was up, I went down to the house of
her mother, and looked upon the goods of
Yash-Noosh, which were piled by the door, —

the goods of Yash-Noosh, a strong hunter who had it in mind to be the father of the children of Unga. Other young men had piled their goods there, and taken them away again; and each young man had made a pile greater than the one before.

" And I laughed to the moon and the stars, and went to my own house where my wealth was stored. And many trips I made, till my pile was greater by the fingers of one hand than the pile of Yash-Noosh. There were fish, dried in the sun and smoked; and forty hides of the hair seal, and half as many of the fur, and each hide was tied at the mouth and big-bellied with oil; and ten skins of bear which I killed in the woods when they came out in the spring. And there were beads and blankets and scarlet cloths, such as I got in trade from the people who lived to the east, and who got them in trade from the people who lived still beyond in the east. And I looked upon the pile of Yash-Noosh and laughed; for I was head man in Akatan, and my wealth was greater than the wealth of all my young men, and my fathers had done deeds, and given laws, and put their names for all time in the mouths of the people.

"So, when the morning came, I went down to the beach, casting out of the corner of my eye at the house of the mother of Unga. My offer yet stood untouched. And the women smiled, and said sly things one to the other. I wondered, for never had such a price been offered; and that night I added more to the pile, and put beside it a kayak of well-tanned skins which never yet had swam in the sea. But in the day it was yet there, open to the laughter of all men. The mother of Unga was crafty, and I grew angry at the shame in which I stood before my people. So that night I added till it became a great pile, and I hauled up my oomiak, which was of the value of twenty kayaks. And in the morning there was no pile.

"Then made I preparation for the wedding, and the people that lived even to the east came for the food of the feast and the *potlach* token. Unga was older than I by the age of four suns in the way we reckoned the years. I was only a stripling; but then I was a chief, and the son of a chief, and it did not matter.

"But a ship shoved her sails above the floor of the ocean, and grew larger with the breath of the wind. From her scuppers she ran clear water, and the men were in haste and worked hard at the pumps. On the bow stood a mighty man, watching the depth of the water and giving commands with a voice of thunder. His eyes were of the pale blue of the deep waters, and his head was maned like that of a sea lion. And his hair was yellow, like the straw of a southern harvest or the manila rope-yarns which sailormen plait.

"Of late years we had seen ships from afar, but this was the first to come to the beach of Akatan. The feast was broken, and the women and children fled to the houses, while we men strung our bows and waited with spears in hand. But when the ship's forefoot smelt the beach the strange men took no notice of us, being busy with their own work. With the falling of the tide they careened the schooner and patched a great hole in her bottom. So the women crept back, and the feast went on.

"When the tide rose, the sea wanderers kedged the schooner to deep water, and then came among us. They bore presents and were friendly; so I made room for them, and out of the largeness of my heart gave them tokens such as I gave all the guests; for it was my wedding day, and I was head man in Akatan. And he with the mane of the sea lion was there, so tall and strong that one looked to see the earth shake with the fall of his feet. He looked much and straight at Unga, with his arms folded, so, and stayed till the sun went away and the stars came out. Then he went down to his ship. After that I took Unga by the hand and led her to my own house. And there was singing and great laughter, and the women said sly things, after the manner of women at such times. But we did not care. Then the people left us alone and went home.

"The last noise had not died away, when the chief of the sea wanderers came in by the door. And he had with him black bottles, from which we drank and made merry. You see, I was only a stripling, and had lived all my days on the edge of the world. So my blood became as fire, and my heart as light as the froth that flies from the surf to the cliff. Unga sat silent among the skins in the corner, her eyes wide, for she seemed to fear. And he with the mane of the sea lion looked upon her straight and long. Then his men came in with bundles of goods, and he piled

before me wealth such as was not in all Akatan.   There were guns, both large and small,
and powder and shot and shell, and bright
axes and knives of steel, and cunning tools,
and strange things the like of which I had
never seen.   When he showed me by sign
that it was all mine, I thought him a great
man to be so free; but he showed me also
that Unga was to go away with him in his
ship.   Do you understand ? — that Unga was
to go away with him in his ship.   The blood
of my fathers flamed hot on the sudden, and
I made to drive him through with my spear.
But the spirit of the bottles had stolen the
life from my arm, and he took me by the neck,
so, and knocked my head against the wall of
the house.   And I was made weak like a newborn child, and my legs would no more stand
under me.   Unga screamed, and she laid hold
of the things of the house with her hands, till
they fell all about us as he dragged her to the
door.   Then he took her in his great arms,
and when she tore at his yellow hair laughed
with a sound like that of the big bull seal in
the rut.

"I crawled to the beach and called upon
my people ; but they were afraid.   Only Yash-

Noosh was a man, and they struck him on the head with an oar, till he lay with his face in the sand and did not move. And they raised the sails to the sound of their songs, and the ship went away on the wind.

"The people said it was good, for there would be no more war of the bloods in Akatan ; but I said never a word, waiting till the time of the full moon, when I put fish and oil in my kayak, and went away to the east. I saw many islands and many people, and I, who had lived on the edge, saw that the world was very large. I talked by signs ; but they had not seen a schooner nor a man with the mane of a sea lion, and they pointed always to the east. And I slept in queer places, and ate odd things, and met strange faces. Many laughed, for they thought me light of head ; but sometimes old men turned my face to the light and blessed me, and the eyes of the young women grew soft as they asked me of the strange ship, and Unga, and the men of the sea.

"And in this manner, through rough seas and great storms, I came to Unalaska. There were two schooners there, but neither was the one I sought. So I passed on to the east,

with the world growing ever larger, and in
the Island of Unamok there was no word of
the ship, nor in Kadiak, nor in Atognak.
And so I came one day to a rocky land,
where men dug great holes in the mountain.
And there was a schooner, but not my
schooner, and men loaded upon it the rocks
which they dug. This I thought childish,
for all the world was made of rocks; but they
gave me food and set me to work. When
the schooner was deep in the water, the captain gave me money and told me to go; but
I asked which way he went, and he pointed
south. I made signs that I would go with
him; and he laughed at first, but then, being
short of men, took me to help work the ship.
So I came to talk after their manner, and to
heave on ropes, and to reef the stiff sails in
sudden squalls, and to take my turn at the
wheel. But it was not strange, for the blood
of my fathers was the blood of the men of
the sea.

"I had thought it an easy task to find him
I sought, once I got among his own people;
and when we raised the land one day, and
passed between a gateway of the sea to a
port, I looked for perhaps as many schooners

as there were fingers to my hands. But the
ships lay against the wharves for miles, packed
like so many little fish; and when I went
among them to ask for a man with the mane
of a sea lion, they laughed, and answered me
in the tongues of many peoples. And I
found that they hailed from the uttermost
parts of the earth.

" And I went into the city to look upon
the face of every man. But they were like
the cod when they run thick on the banks,
and I could not count them. And the noise
smote upon me till I could not hear, and my
head was dizzy with much movement. So I
went on and on, through the lands which
sang in the warm sunshine; where the har-
vests lay rich on the plains; and where great
cities were fat with men that lived like
women, with false words in their mouths and
their hearts black with the lust of gold. And
all the while my people of Akatan hunted
and fished, and were happy in the thought
that the world was small.

" But the look in the eyes of Unga coming
home from the fishing was with me always,
and I knew I would find her when the time
was met. She walked down quiet lanes in

the dusk of the evening, or led me chases
across the thick fields wet with the morning
dew, and there was a promise in her eyes
such as only the woman Unga could give.

" So I wandered through a thousand cities.
Some were gentle and gave me food, and
others laughed, and still others cursed; but I
kept my tongue between my teeth, and went
strange ways and saw strange sights. Sometimes, I, who was a chief and the son of a
chief, toiled for men, — men rough of speech
and hard as iron, who wrung gold from the
sweat and sorrow of their fellow men. Yet
no word did I get of my quest, till I came
back to the sea like a homing seal to the
rookeries. But this was at another port, in
another country which lay to the north. And
there I heard dim tales of the yellow-haired
sea wanderer, and I learned that he was a
hunter of seals, and that even then he was
abroad on the ocean.

" So I shipped on a seal schooner with the
lazy Siwashes, and followed his trackless trail
to the north where the hunt was then warm.
And we were away weary months, and spoke
many of the fleet, and heard much of the wild
doings of him I sought ; but never once did

we raise him above the sea.   We went north, even to the Pribyloffs, and killed the seals in herds on the beach, and brought their warm bodies aboard till our scuppers ran grease and blood and no man could stand upon the deck.   Then were we chased by a ship of slow steam, which fired upon us with great guns.   But we put on sail till the sea was over our decks and washed them clean, and lost ourselves in a fog.

"It is said, at this time, while we fled with fear at our hearts, that the yellow-haired sea wanderer put into the Pribyloffs, right to the factory, and while the part of his men held the servants of the company, the rest loaded ten thousand green skins from the salt-houses.   I say it is said, but I believe ; for in the voyages I made on the coast with never a meeting, the northern seas rang with his wildness and daring, till the three nations which have lands there sought him with their ships. And I heard of Unga, for the captains sang loud in her praise, and she was always with him.   She had learned the ways of his people, they said, and was happy.   But I knew better, — knew that her heart harked back to her own people by the yellow beach of Akatan.

"So, after a long time, I went back to the port which is by a gateway of the sea, and there I learned that he had gone across the girth of the great ocean to hunt for the seal to the east of the warm land which runs south from the Russian Seas. And I, who was become a sailorman, shipped with men of his own race, and went after him in the hunt of the seal. And there were few ships off that new land ; but we hung on the flank of the seal pack and harried it north through all the spring of the year. And when the cows were heavy with pup and crossed the Russian line, our men grumbled and were afraid. For there was much fog, and every day men were lost in the boats. They would not work, so the captain turned the ship back toward the way it came. But I knew the yellow-haired sea wanderer was unafraid, and would hang by the pack, even to the Russian Isles, where few men go. So I took a boat, in the black of night, when the lookout dozed on the fok'slehead, and went alone to the warm, long land. And I journeyed south to meet the men by Yeddo Bay, who are wild and unafraid. And the Yoshiwara girls were small, and bright like steel, and good to look upon ; but I could not stop, for I knew that Unga rolled on the tossing floor by the rookeries of the north.

" The men by Yeddo Bay had met from the ends of the earth, and had neither gods nor homes, sailing under the flag of the Japanese. And with them I went to the rich beaches of Copper Island, where our salt-piles became high with skins. And in that silent sea we saw no man till we were ready to come away. Then, one day, the fog lifted on the edge of a heavy wind, and there jammed down upon us a schooner, with close in her wake the cloudy funnels of a Russian man-of-war. We fled away on the beam of the wind, with the schooner jamming still closer and plunging ahead three feet to our two. And upon her poop was the man with the mane of the sea lion, pressing the rails under with the canvas and laughing in his strength of life. And Unga was there, — I knew her on the moment, — but he sent her below when the cannons began to talk across the sea. As I say, with three feet to our two, till we saw the rudder lift green at every jump, — and I swinging on to the wheel and cursing, with my back to the Russian shot. For we knew he had it in mind to run before us, that he might get away while we were caught. And they knocked our masts out of us till we dragged into the wind like a wounded gull; but he went on over the edge of the sky-line, — he and Unga.

" What could we? The fresh hides spoke for themselves. So they took us to a Russian port, and after that to a lone country, where they set us to work in the mines to dig salt. And some died, and — and some did not die."

Naass swept the blanket from his shoulders, disclosing the gnarled and twisted flesh, marked with the unmistakable striations of the knout. Prince hastily covered him, for it was not nice to look upon.

" We were there a weary time; and sometimes men got away to the south, but they always came back. So, when we who hailed from Yeddo Bay rose in the night and took the guns from the guards, we went to the north. And the land was very large, with plains, soggy with water, and great forests. And the cold came, with much snow on the ground, and no man knew the way. Weary months we journeyed through the endless forest, — I do not remember, now, for there was little food and often we lay down to die. But at last we came to the cold sea, and but three were left to look upon it. One had shipped from Yeddo as captain, and he knew in his head the lay of the great lands, and of the place where men may cross from one to the other on the ice. And he led us, — I do not know, it was so long, — till there were but two. When we came to that place we found five of the strange people which live in that country, and they had dogs and skins, and we were very poor. We fought in the snow till they died, and the captain died, and the dogs and skins were mine. Then I crossed on the ice, which was broken, and once I drifted till a gale from the west put me upon the shore. And after that, Golovin Bay, Pastilik, and the priest. Then south, south, to the warm sunlands where first I wandered.

"But the sea was no longer fruitful, and those who went upon it after the seal went to little profit and great risk. The fleets scattered, and the captains and the men had no word of those I sought. So I turned away from the ocean which never rests, and went among the lands, where the trees, the houses, and the mountains sit always in one place and do not move. I journeyed far, and came to learn many things, even to the way of reading and writing from books. It was well I should do this, for it came upon me that Unga must know these things, and that some day, when the time was met — we — you understand, when the time was met.

"So I drifted, like those little fish which raise a sail to the wind, but cannot steer. But my eyes and my ears were open always, and I went among men who traveled much, for I knew they had but to see those I sought, to remember. At last there came a man, fresh from the mountains, with pieces of rock in which the free gold stood to the size of peas, and he had heard, he had met, he knew them. They were rich, he said, and lived in the place where they drew the gold from the ground.

"It was in a wild country, and very far away; but in time I came to the camp, hidden between the mountains, where men worked night and day, out of the sight of the sun. Yet the time was not come. I listened to the talk of the people. He had

gone away, — they had gone away, — to
England, it was said, in the matter of bringing men with much money together to form
companies. I saw the house they had lived
in; more like a palace, such as one sees in
the old countries. In the nighttime I crept
in through a window that I might see in
what manner he treated her. I went from
room to room, and in such way thought
kings and queens must live, it was all so
very good. And they all said he treated her
like a queen, and many marveled as to what
breed of woman she was; for there was other
blood in her veins, and she was different from
the women of Akatan, and no one knew her
for what she was. Ay, she was a queen; but
I was a chief, and the son of a chief, and I
had paid for her an untold price of skin and
boat and bead.

"But why so many words? I was a sailorman, and knew the way of the ships on the
seas. I followed to England, and then to
other countries. Sometimes I heard of them
by word of mouth, sometimes I read of them
in the papers; yet never once could I come
by them, for they had much money, and
traveled fast, while I was a poor man. Then

came trouble upon them, and their wealth slipped away, one day, like a curl of smoke. The papers were full of it at the time; but after that nothing was said, and I knew they had gone back where more gold could be got from the ground.

"They had dropped out of the world, being now poor; and so I wandered from camp to camp, even north to the Kootenay Country, where I picked up the cold scent. They had come and gone, some said this way, and some that, and still others that they had gone to the Country of the Yukon. And I went this way, and I went that, ever journeying from place to place, till it seemed I must grow weary of the world which was so large. But in the Kootenay I traveled a bad trail, and a long trail, with a ' breed ' of the Northwest, who saw fit to die when the famine pinched. He had been to the Yukon by an unknown way over the mountains, and when he knew his time was near gave me the map and the secret of a place where he swore by his gods there was much gold.

"After that all the world began to flock into the north. I was a poor man; I sold myself to be a driver of dogs. The rest you know. I met him and her in Dawson. She did not know me, for I was only a stripling, and her life had been large, so she had no time to remember the one who had paid for her an untold price.

"So? You bought me from my term of service. I went back to bring things about in my own way; for I had waited long, and now that I had my hand upon him was in no hurry. As I say, I had it in mind to do my own way; for I read back in my life, through all I had seen and suffered, and remembered the cold and hunger of the endless forest by the Russian Seas. As you know, I led him into the east, — him and Unga, — into the east where many have gone and few returned. I led them to the spot where the bones and the curses of men lie with the gold which they may not have.

"The way was long and the trail unpacked. Our dogs were many and ate much; nor could our sleds carry till the break of spring. We must come back before the river ran free. So here and there we cached grub, that our sleds might be lightened and there be no chance of famine on the back trip. At the McQuestion there were three men, and near

them we built a cache, as also did we at
the Mayo, where was a hunting-camp of a
dozen Pellys which had crossed the divide
from the south. After that, as we went on
into the east, we saw no men; only the sleeping river, the moveless forest, and the White
Silence of the North. As I say, the way was
long and the trail unpacked. Sometimes, in
a day's toil, we made no more than eight
miles, or ten, and at night we slept like dead
men. And never once did they dream that
I was Naass, head man of Akatan, the righter
of wrongs.

"We now made smaller caches, and in the
nighttime it was a small matter to go back on
the trail we had broken, and change them in
such way that one might deem the wolverines
the thieves. Again, there be places where
there is a fall to the river, and the water is
unruly, and the ice makes above and is eaten
away beneath. In such a spot the sled I
drove broke through, and the dogs; and to
him and Unga it was ill luck, but no more.
And there was much grub on that sled, and
the dogs the strongest. But he laughed, for
he was strong of life, and gave the dogs that
were left little grub till we cut them from the

harnesses, one by one, and fed them to their mates. We would go home light, he said, traveling and eating from cache to cache, with neither dogs nor sleds; which was true, for our grub was very short, and the last dog died in the traces the night we came to the gold and the bones and the curses of men.

" To reach that place, — and the map spoke true, — in the heart of the great mountains, we cut ice steps against the wall of a divide. One looked for a valley beyond, but there was no valley; the snow spread away, level as the great harvest plains, and here and there about us mighty mountains shoved their white heads among the stars. And midway on that strange plain which should have been a valley, the earth and the snow fell away, straight down toward the heart of the world. Had we not been sailormen our heads would have swung round with the sight; but we stood on the dizzy edge that we might see a way to get down. And on one side, and one side only, the wall had fallen away till it was like the slope of the decks in a topsail breeze. I do not know why this thing should be so, but it was so.

Midway on that strange plain the
earth and snow fell away.

' It is the mouth of hell,' he said; ' let us go down.' And we went down.

" And on the bottom there was a cabin, built by some man, of logs which he had cast down from above. It was a very old cabin; for men had died there alone at different times, and on pieces of birch bark which were there we read their last words and their curses. One had died of scurvy; another's partner had robbed him of his last grub and powder and stolen away; a third had been mauled by a bald-face grizzly; a fourth had hunted for game and starved, — and so it went, and they had been loath to leave the gold, and had died by the side of it in one way or another. And the worthless gold they had gathered yellowed the floor of the cabin like in a dream.

" But his soul was steady, and his head clear, this man I had led thus far. ' We have nothing to eat,' he said, 'and we will only look upon this gold, and see whence it comes and how much there be. Then we will go away quick, before it gets into our eyes and steals away our judgment. And in this way we may return in the end, with more grub, and possess it all.' So we looked upon the great vein, which cut the wall of the pit as a true vein should; and we measured it, and traced it from above and below, and drove the stakes of the claims and blazed the trees in token of our rights. Then, our knees shaking with lack of food, and a sickness in our bellies, and our hearts chugging close to our mouths, we climbed the mighty wall for the last time and turned our faces to the back trip.

"The last stretch we dragged Unga between us, and we fell often, but in the end we made the cache. And lo, there was no grub. It was well done, for he thought it the wolverines, and damned them and his gods in the one breath. But Unga was brave, and smiled, and put her hand in his, till I turned away that I might hold myself. 'We will rest by the fire,' she said, 'till morning, and we will gather strength from our moccasins.' So we cut the tops of our moccasins in strips, and boiled them half of the night, that we might chew them and swallow them. And in the morning we talked of our chance. The next cache was five days' journey; we could not make it. We must find game.

" ' We will go forth and hunt,' he said.

" ' Yes,' said I, ' we will go forth and hunt.'

" And he ruled that Unga stay by the fire and save her strength. And we went forth, he in quest of the moose, and I to the cache I had changed. But I ate little, so they might not see in me much strength. And in the night he fell many times as he drew into camp. And I too made to suffer great weakness, stumbling over my snow-shoes as though each step might be my last. And we gathered strength from our moccasins.

" He was a great man. His soul lifted his body to the last; nor did he cry aloud, save for the sake of Unga. On the second day I followed him, that I might not miss the end. And he lay down to rest often. That night he was near gone ; but in the morning he swore weakly and went forth again. He was like a drunken man, and I looked many times for him to give up ; but his was the strength of the strong, and his soul the soul of a giant, for he lifted his body through all the weary day. And he shot two ptarmigan, but would not eat them. He needed no fire ;

they meant life; but his thought was for Unga, and he turned toward camp. He no longer walked, but crawled on hand and knee through the snow. I came to him, and read death in his eyes. Even then it was not too late to eat of the ptarmigan. He cast away his rifle, and carried the birds in his mouth like a dog. I walked by his side, upright. And he looked at me during the moments he rested, and wondered that I was so strong. I could see it, though he no longer spoke; and when his lips moved, they moved without sound. As I say, he was a great man, and my heart spoke for softness; but I read back in my life, and remembered the cold and hunger of the endless forest by the Russian Seas. Besides, Unga was mine, and I had paid for her an untold price of skin and boat and bead.

"And in this manner we came through the white forest, with the silence heavy upon us like a damp sea mist. And the ghosts of the past were in the air and all about us; and I saw the yellow beach of Akatan, and the kayaks racing home from the fishing, and the houses on the rim of the forest. And the men who had made themselves chiefs

were there, the lawgivers whose blood I bore,
and whose blood I had wedded in Unga. Ay,
and Yash-Noosh walked with me, the wet
sand in his hair, and his war spear, broken
as he fell upon it, still in his hand. And I
knew the time was met, and saw in the eyes
of Unga the promise.

"As I say, we came thus through the forest, till the smell of the camp smoke was in
our nostrils. And I bent above him, and
tore the ptarmigan from his teeth. He
turned on his side and rested, the wonder
mounting in his eyes, and the hand which
was under slipping slow toward the knife at
his hip. But I took it from him, smiling
close in his face. Even then he did not
understand. So I made to drink from black
bottles, and to build high upon the snow a
pile of goods, and to live again the things
which happened on the night of my marriage.
I spoke no word, but he understood. Yet
was he unafraid. There was a sneer to his
lips, and cold anger, and he gathered new
strength with the knowledge. It was not
far, but the snow was deep, and he dragged
himself very slow. Once, he lay so long, I
turned him over and gazed into his eyes.

And sometimes he looked forth, and sometimes death. And when I loosed him he struggled on again. In this way we came to the fire. Unga was at his side on the instant. His lips moved, without sound; then he pointed at me, that Unga might understand. And after that he lay in the snow, very still, for a long while. Even now is he there in the snow.

"I said no word till I had cooked the ptarmigan. Then I spoke to her, in her own tongue, which she had not heard in many years. She straightened herself, so, and her eyes were wonder-wide, and she asked who I was, and where I had learned that speech.

"'I am Naass,' I said.

"'You?' she said. 'You?' And she crept close that she might look upon me.

"'Yes,' I answered; 'I am Naass, head man of Akatan, the last of the blood, as you are the last of the blood.'

"And she laughed. By all the things I have seen and the deeds I have done, may I never hear such a laugh again. It put the chill to my soul, sitting there in the White Silence, alone with death and this woman who laughed.

"'Come!' I said, for I thought she wandered. 'Eat of the food and let us be gone. It is a far fetch from here to Akatan.'

"But she shoved her face in his yellow mane, and laughed till it seemed the heavens must fall about our ears. I had thought she would be overjoyed at the sight of me, and eager to go back to the memory of old times; but this seemed a strange form to take.

"'Come!' I cried, taking her strong by the hand. 'The way is long and dark. Let us hurry!'

"'Where?' she asked, sitting up, and ceasing from her strange mirth.

"'To Akatan,' I answered, intent on the light to grow on her face at the thought. But it became like his, with a sneer to the lips, and cold anger.

"'Yes,' she said; 'we will go, hand in hand, to Akatan, you and I. And we will live in the dirty huts, and eat of the fish and oil, and bring forth a spawn, — a spawn to be proud of all the days of our life. We will forget the world and be happy, very happy. It is good, most good. Come! Let us hurry. Let us go back to Akatan.'

"And she ran her hand through his yellow hair, and smiled in a way which was not good. And there was no promise in her eyes.

"I sat silent, and marveled at the strangeness of woman. I went back to the night when he dragged her from me, and she screamed and tore at his hair, — at his hair which now she played with and would not leave. Then I remembered the price and the long years of waiting; and I gripped her close, and dragged her away as he had done. And she held back, even as on that night, and fought like a she-cat for its whelp. And when the fire was between us and the man, I loosed her, and she sat and listened. And I told her of all that lay between, of all that had happened me on strange seas, of all that I had done in strange lands; of my weary quest, and the hungry years, and the promise which had been mine from the first. Ay, I told all, even to what had passed that day between the man and me, and in the days yet young. And as I spoke I saw the promise grow in her eyes, full and large like the break of dawn. And I read pity there, the tenderness of woman, the love, the heart and the soul of Unga. And I was a stripling again, for the look was the look of Unga as

she ran up the beach, laughing, to the home
of her mother. The stern unrest was gone,
and the hunger, and the weary waiting. The
time was met. I felt the call of her breast,
and it seemed there I must pillow my head
and forget. She opened her arms to me, and
I came against her. Then, sudden, the hate
flamed in her eye, her hand was at my hip.
And once, twice, she passed the knife.

"'Dog!' she sneered, as she flung me into
the snow. 'Swine!' And then she laughed
till the silence cracked, and went back to her
dead.

"As I say, once she passed the knife, and
twice; but she was weak with hunger, and it
was not meant that I should die. Yet was I
minded to stay in that place, and to close my
eyes in the last long sleep with those whose
lives had crossed with mine and led my feet
on unknown trails. But there lay a debt
upon me which would not let me rest.

"And the way was long, the cold bitter, and
there was little grub. The Pellys had found
no moose, and had robbed my cache. And
so had the three white men; but they lay
thin and dead in their cabin as I passed.
After that I do not remember, till I came

here, and found food and fire, — much fire."

As he finished, he crouched closely, even jealously, over the stove. For a long while the slush-lamp shadows played tragedies upon the wall.

"But Unga!" cried Prince, the vision still strong upon him.

"Unga? She would not eat of the ptarmigan. She lay with her arms about his neck, her face deep in his yellow hair. I drew the fire close, that she might not feel the frost; but she crept to the other side. And I built a fire there; yet it was little good, for she would not eat. And in this manner they still lie up there in the snow."

"And you?" asked Malemute Kid.

"I do not know; but Akatan is small, and I have little wish to go back and live on the edge of the world. Yet is there small use in life. I can go to Constantine, and he will put irons upon me, and one day they will tie a piece of rope, so, and I will sleep good. Yet — no; I do not know."

"But, Kid," protested Prince, "this is murder!"

"Hush!" commanded Malemute Kid.

"There be things greater than our wisdom, beyond our justice. The right and the wrong of this we cannot say, and it is not for us to judge."

Naass drew yet closer to the fire. There was a great silence, and in each man's eyes many pictures came and went.